ATLAS
SHADOWRIDGE GUARDIANS MC

BECCA JAMESON

PHOTOGRAPHY BY
TONYA CLARK PHOTOGRAPHY

COVER MODEL
THOMAS HOSTETLER

Copyright © 2023 by Becca Jameson

All characters and events in this book are fictitious. And resemblance to actual persons living or dead is strictly coincidental.

All rights reserved.

No part of this book may be reproduced in any form or by any electronic or mechanical means, including information storage and retrieval systems, without written permission from the author, except for the use of brief quotations in a book review.

❀ Created with Vellum

ABOUT SHADOWRIDGE GUARDIANS MC

Combining the sizzling talents of bestselling authors Pepper North, Kate Oliver, and Becca Jameson, the Shadowridge Guardians are guaranteed to give you a thrill and leave you dreaming of your own throbbing motorcycle joyride.

Are you daring enough to ride with a club of rough, growly, commanding men? The protective Daddies of the Shadowridge Guardians Motorcycle Club will stop at nothing to ensure the safety and protection of everything that belongs to them: their Littles, their club, and their town. Throw in some sassy, naughty, mischievous women who won't hesitate to serve their fair share of attitude even in the face of looming danger, and this brand new MC Romance series is ready to ignite!

Shadowridge Guardians MC
Steele
Kade
Atlas
Doc
Gabriel

ABOUT SHADOWRIDGE GUARDIANS MC

Talon
Bear
Faust
Storm

Atlas

"Baby girl, I'm going to count to three..."

Carlee is doing just fine on her own. She doesn't need a man in her life. They never treat her right anyway. She certainly doesn't need her best friend's brother to swoop into town and take over like he never left her. It takes him less than one day to cause her to lose her car, her job, and her apartment. Now she's furious.

Atlas is in town as a favor to his father to help the MC club. What he's not prepared for is Carlee—a woman he's spent years trying to forget. A woman with cute pigtails, a sassy attitude, a pile of problems, and the need for a good spanking.

She can push him away all she wants, but he won't leave town until she can stand on her own.

CHAPTER ONE

Two high bouncy pigtails.

That was the first thing he saw from the beam of his headlight as he pulled his bike over to the side of the road behind her car. Less than a second later, he took in her amazing ass encased in perfect form-fitting jeans. She was standing at her open trunk, leaning over the edge. She was short enough that whatever she was trying to reach deep in the trunk made her rise up on her tiptoes.

Damn, she was sexy.

Atlas swallowed hard as he turned off his bike, kicked out the stand, and removed his helmet. He set it on the seat after swinging his leg over the top. She hadn't glanced over her shoulder yet, which was strange. She had to have heard his noisy bike in addition to the fact that his headlight was powerful and fully illuminating her fantastic ass and everything around her. But he was off the bike and heading toward her before she finally turned around.

She held a hand up to shield her eyes from the beam of light, shoulders dropping. Her other hand went to her hip.

Odd.

"Do you need some help?" Atlas asked.

She said nothing until he was close enough to finally make out her features. And then she gasped as she dropped her hand when his body blocked the bright light. "Atlas?"

Big wide brown eyes stared up at him. Even though it had been a long time since he'd last seen her, he knew those eyes. "Carlee?"

"What are you doing in town?" She folded her hands in front of her and rocked back and forth on her tennis shoes.

He drank her in from head to toe. In addition to the adorable messy pigtails, she had on a pink T-shirt that fit snug over her breasts, making it impossible for him to avoid noticing her perfect round, pert tits. They weren't more than a handful, and her shirt was thin enough that he could see the lace of her bra beneath.

He'd already admired her fantastic ass from behind before he'd known who he was lusting after. Her jeans were tight on her slender frame. Her tennis shoes were also pink, though they were worn and scuffed.

"I'm here to help the club. Apparently the treasurer took off. My dad asked me to come make sense of the books." He nodded toward her car after his brief explanation. "Car trouble?"

She winced and then lifted a hand to rub her forehead. "Yeah. It's a piece of shit, but it's all I can afford, so…"

"How about if I take a look?"

"I wouldn't want to put you out. I'm sure you have better things to do. I'll just…" She tucked her full lower lip in between her teeth and chewed on it.

"You'll just what? Why were you standing on the side of the road in the dark rummaging through your trunk, Carlee?" He realized the tone of his voice was gruff, but he couldn't help it. She shouldn't have gotten out of her car. She should have locked it and called a club member to come help her.

Any member of the Shadowridge Guardians MC would have been here in a heartbeat to help her. Hell, she'd been hanging around the club from the time she was a little girl. He'd known her all that time too. After all, his sister, Remi, was her best friend.

She was certainly not a child anymore. She was twenty-five. He hadn't seen her in years. Part of him felt like a pervert for lusting after her, but fuck, she was a grown adult. And from the looks of it, Little. That possibility alone made his cock jump to attention. Atlas hadn't played with a Little in a long time.

You're not playing with this one either. Remi would have a fit, plus there was no way Carlee thought of him like that. And, he was only in town for a month. Not one day longer.

Carlee lowered her gaze and mumbled, "I was looking for a recyclable grocery bag. I thought I had one in the trunk."

He stepped closer. "What for? It's not safe out here. It's dark. You should have stayed in your car."

She took a step back, rubbing her palms together. "I was going to walk. I just wanted to tuck my things into a bag so they wouldn't get stolen."

"Walk?" he nearly shouted. "Carlee, whatever for?"

She flinched and lifted her gaze. "Don't shout at me." Her eyebrows were drawn together in a fierce expression, but her eyes were watery as if she was about to cry.

He blew out a breath, feeling like a shit. "I'm sorry." He tried to control his frustration. He needed to listen to her. "Explain why you didn't call the club." The Guardians lived for rescuing damsels in distress. She was practically an honorary member. This made no sense.

She swallowed. "I don't have my phone, and for your information, I wouldn't have called the club anyway." She leaned into him as she made this declaration. "I can take care of myself. I don't need help."

Both his brows rose high on his forehead, and it took every-thing in him to avoid losing his temper. This Little girl needed a lecture about safety, and it needed to be accompanied by a firm spanking.

He decided to address one issue at a time. "Where is your phone?"

"In my apartment. It's dead, and I lost the charger," she murmured.

He had a hand over his face. He was tempted to turn her around, lean her over the trunk of her car, and swat her ass right here. But he couldn't do that, of course. She wasn't his. "That's not safe, Carlee. You shouldn't go anywhere without your phone. What if your car broke down?" He tipped his head toward her and pointed at her car to emphasize his point.

She rolled her eyes, which did nothing to alleviate his need to spank her. Her hands went to her hips. "For your information, Mr. High and Mighty, not all of us are made of fucking money. My phone isn't working. Charging it won't help. I can't afford a new one. Are you happy?"

He winced. Shit.

"And," she continued, as if now that the floodgates were open, she had found the spine to let it all out, "if you must know, I'm not hanging around the club these days, so I would have walked even if I had the fanciest phone on earth. And last I checked, you're still a member of the club even though you moved away, so if you don't mind stepping out of my way, I'm going to walk home."

She spun around, slammed the trunk shut, and skirted him to reach into the front seat of her car. The door had been standing open. She leaned in so far that it was impossible to ignore her fine ass yet again.

It took her several seconds of rummaging before she eased back out. She had several items in her hand, and she stuffed them all in a plastic grocery sack. He didn't miss the worn stuffie that got carefully placed on top. He couldn't quite make out what it was. Maybe a hamster or a mouse? It wasn't very large.

Atlas couldn't imagine why she was on the outs with the club, but he sure as shit wasn't going to let her walk anywhere. She was high if she thought that would happen in a million years.

"You're not walking, Carlee," he informed her, holding out a hand. "Let me tuck your things in the saddlebag. I'll take you home."

"I'll be fine," she reiterated without meeting his gaze. She shut her car door, locked it, and tucked the keys in her worn, oversized purse. With the purse strapped across her shoulder and the plastic bag in her hand, she turned away from him.

He didn't let her get two steps before he snagged her free hand and stopped her. "Carlee Deveraux, I don't have a clue what's going on with you, Little girl, but I'm about five seconds from spanking your cute little ass to knock some sense into you. Would you like to climb onto my bike willingly so I can drive you home? Or would you like me to spank you here on the side of the road before you climb onto my bike so I can drive you home?"

She gasped, as expected. "You can't Daddy me, Atlas Monroe. I'm not *your* Little girl. I'm not anyone's Little girl."

He slid his hand up her arm to her bicep. "So you admit you're Little though." He wasn't asking. He was pointing out the obvious. He might have intentionally manipulated her into admitting that fact.

She groaned.

He pointed toward his bike with his free hand. "Which is it going to be?"

Her shoulders dropped. "If I let you take me home, will you drop me off and leave without hassling me further?"

"Nope. Not a chance. I have about a dozen questions I want answers to. You're going to provide them. When I'm satisfied with your responses and your safety, then I'll consider leaving you to sleep." As a Daddy, he couldn't conscientiously leave her without checking off that list of items no matter what. But Carlee wasn't just any Little. She was someone he knew. Someone he was suddenly extremely attracted to.

"Atlas..." she whined.

She had no idea how fucking hot she was right now, all riled up, pouting, arguing, and whining. His cock was growing harder by the moment—for this woman he hadn't seen in so long he was still wrapping his head around the fact that she was no longer a teenager. He should have been able to process that. After all, Remi was her same age.

"Do I need to count to three? Or maybe the reason you're arguing with me is because you would prefer I swat your bottom right here. Is that it?" He was half kidding, but it was possible that was exactly what she wanted and needed.

She gasped. "You are *not* spanking me. Not here or anywhere. Forget it." She did, however, twist around and stomp toward his bike.

It was hard not to smirk as he followed her. Without a word, he took her grocery sack from her hand and opened the saddlebag to tuck it inside. Something was already in the saddlebag though, and he lifted it out to find it was an adorable stuffed bear.

Carlee was staring at him when he glanced at her.

He smirked. "Wonder how this little fellow got in my saddlebag," he mused.

"Man, you have been gone a long time," Carlee grumbled.

He met her gaze again. "What'd I miss?"

"All your brothers carry teddy bears in their saddlebags just in case they encounter a damsel in distress. Or more specifically a Little."

"Really?" He grinned. What a nice idea. "I guess even though my bike was in storage until today, someone stuck it in there for me." He suddenly held it out to her. "I'd say you fit the description. Damsel in distress." He leaned in closer. "Little too."

She balked, not taking it. "You should keep it. I'm not distressed, and I'm not your Little."

Atlas narrowed his gaze. "You didn't say the damsel had to be *my* Little. And you are about as distressed as a Little girl could possibly be." He continued to hold it out to her.

She stared at it for long seconds before snatching it from his hand and then stuffing it into the plastic bag next to what was definitely a hamster. "Fine. Whatever."

Atlas smirked to himself as he tucked everything into the saddlebag before he pulled his helmet over her head. It was a bit large but it would work in a pinch.

He'd only been in town a few hours. He'd barely reacquainted himself with his bike yet. In fact, he'd been out for this ride so he could clear his head and remind himself how good it felt to have the power of the engine beneath him. Normally he wouldn't travel without a spare helmet in a town filled with more than its fair share of Littles, but his bike had come out of storage hours ago. It wasn't decked out for visitors yet.

Carlee stared at him. "You don't have a spare helmet?"

"No. I'm ill-prepared. It won't happen again. I promise."

She narrowed her gaze. "This is the one and only ride I'm ever taking with you, Atlas, so don't outfit your bike with a spare helmet on my account." She started to lift it off her head. "You wear it. It's too big on me anyway."

He stopped her by tugging her hands out of the way and cinching the chin strap as tight as he could. "I'll drive slowly." Why did it annoy him so much that she so adamantly insisted she wouldn't be riding with him again?

She was mistaken. Of that he was certain. This Little girl was going to be spending some time on the back of his bike for at least a few days. After all, she didn't have a car. She would surely need a lift to wherever she worked until he could get her car sorted out.

Atlas swung his leg over his bike and settled before reaching out a hand. "Climb on."

She sighed dramatically before taking his hand, planting her foot on the footrest, and tossing her leg over. She immediately situated herself so she was hardly touching him, her grip on the sides of the seat at her hips.

Atlas twisted his head around, brow lifted. "Carlee Marie Deveraux, if you won't wrap your arms around me and hold on tight, I'm not moving an inch. What on earth has gotten into you? It's not safe riding behind me without holding on."

She stared at him for several seconds before finally releasing the seat to set her hands on his hips. "Don't call me by my full name like I've misbehaved," she insisted.

He chuckled. "You have misbehaved, Little girl." Atlas grabbed both her hands and pulled them around his waist. She was so much smaller than him that she could barely connect her fingers together, but he'd be damned if he let her lean away from him.

Perhaps he was being a bit highhanded, but he would insist that any woman at his back on his bike grip him tight, especially a Little girl.

There were a few things Atlas knew to be true.

Carlee was most definitely a Little.

And dammit, but she was tugging at his heartstrings.

He didn't have the luxury of falling for her or taking over her life. He was only here for one month. Not a day longer. It had been hard enough taking a leave of absence from his job. The only reason it had been possible at all was because it was not tax season. He'd told his boss there was a family emergency, and the man hadn't hesitated to give him the needed time.

Atlas hadn't lied. There was a family emergency. The club treasurer, Silver, really had taken off, and no one had seen or heard from him in two weeks. Atlas's father, Rock, had begged Atlas to come home and help out with the books.

Returning his attention to the adorably angry Little girl at his back, Atlas started up the bike. "Where is your apartment?"

When she mumbled the name of the complex, he stiffened. He'd been gone a long time, but not so long that he didn't remember that wasn't a nice part of town. Why was she living in such deplorable conditions? Surely the club could help her out if she was in need of assistance. It was practically their motto.

Atlas intended to find out. "Hold on tight, Carlee."

CHAPTER TWO

hit. Shit shit shit.

What the hell is Atlas Monroe doing in town?

She knew though. Hell, she knew better than most people why Atlas would be in town. She didn't want to fucking talk about it, but she was well aware that Silver had skipped town, leaving the club without a treasurer.

Carlee tried hard not to think about the firm body in front of her. She wouldn't think about how her breasts were plastered to the back of his leather jacket. She would ignore his six-pack abs that flexed every time he leaned with the bike to take another turn. She wouldn't notice how good he smelled or the slight curl of the ends of his hair or the four-day beard he probably kept that way intentionally.

Nope. She was a smart girl. *Do not fall for Atlas Monroe.*

Except it was years too late for that. She'd been half in love with him since she'd been old enough to notice boys. He was eight years older than her, so by the time she was in high school, he was already graduating from college.

Atlas's dad, Rock, had thrown a huge party for him when he'd graduated from college with his finance degree. Rock had been the proudest man on earth that day, and rightfully so. It wasn't every day a club member left the fold, moved to a big city, and earned a degree.

The excitement had been short-lived when Atlas announced he'd taken a job with a large accounting firm and would be moving away for good. Rock had grumbled for months, though the man had to have known this would happen.

Carlee had been heartbroken too, but she'd never mentioned a word to anyone, not even her best friend, Remi, Atlas's sister.

Nope. Carlee had held that shit in, tamped it down. Who would have taken her crush seriously anyway? Certainly not Atlas. He probably hadn't even noticed she'd existed. She'd been fifteen. Nothing more than his baby sister's friend.

She'd seen him from time to time over the years since then, but he'd never stuck around for long. *He isn't going to this time either*, she reminded herself. He was here to clean up a mess, the mess fucking Silver left in his wake. When it was fixed, Atlas would go back to the city.

Carlee wasn't a teenager anymore. She was a grown woman. Twenty-five. She'd led a hard life, but she'd managed to make ends meet on her own, and she would continue to do so.

What she didn't need was to spend time with Atlas while he was in town. That would be detrimental to her sanity. Already the man had a grip on her. The feel of his fingers on hers… The growly sounds he made when he ordered her around… The furrowed brows that meant business…

Yeah, her panties were wet, which infuriated her, and now that she was plastered to his back, her nipples were hard too. Or maybe that was from the chill in the air. The T-shirt had been fine for riding in her car. Not fine for the bike. She had goosebumps. She told herself that's what was affecting her nipples.

Plus there was the lace bra. It was one half of her only sexy bra and panty set. She rarely wore it. She was only wearing it tonight because everything else was dirty.

A part of her was disappointed when he arrived at her apartment building. Their time was over. She wouldn't see him again, but she would always remember these minutes with him. Minutes she'd never expected to get with her arms wrapped around him and her breasts flattened to his back.

She quickly slid to the ground and wrapped her arms around herself against the chill. "Thanks for the ride. It was kind of you." She turned and fled toward the door to the four-story dump.

Breathing hard, she pulled the heavy door open, but before she could step inside, Atlas was on her, holding the door.

There was no way she was going to invite him into her apartment. Not a chance in hell. She didn't want him to know how she lived, nor did she want him to tell anyone else in the club. His father, for one, would have a coronary if he knew how bad things were. He'd want to step in and take care of her. That was the nature of the Shadowridge Guardians. Well, most of them. It certainly didn't include Silver.

"You're not coming up, Atlas," she informed him as she tried to shove him away from the door.

He held up her grocery sack. "You forgot this. I bet you would have been disappointed later without this worn stuffed hamster." He nodded at the brown fuzzy head sticking out the top.

Shit. Carlee snagged the bag from him. "Thanks."

He nodded toward the small, rundown lobby. "I'm coming up, Carlee," he declared. "Which floor are you on?"

She drew in a deep breath. "You don't need to do that, Atlas. I'm fine. Thank you for the lift," she reiterated.

He tucked a finger under her chin and tipped her face back. "This isn't a negotiation, Little girl. I'm coming up. I've never left a woman at her front door and driven off before in my life.

My father taught me better than that. I'm not starting with you."

She chewed on her bottom lip. "Technically, you're not leaving me at my front door. We're inside now."

He'd inched toward her, causing her to shuffle backward, until they were indeed almost at the stairs.

"Carlee," he growled. "The number of reasons why I'm going to spank your bottom is growing by the minute."

She shivered. "You can't spank me," she reminded him.

"Why the hell not?"

"Because I'm not *your* Little girl," she insisted, her back now flat against the door to the stairs. "I'm not anyone's Little."

"Semantics, Little girl. I told you when we got here I was going to want to hear what's going on with you. I meant it. Now, I gave you a choice at the car, and I'll give you the same one here. Would you like me to spank you here in the lobby where anyone might come out of their apartment and see your naked bottom? Or are you going to lead me upstairs to your apartment?"

Her eyes went wide. Was he serious? Surely not. He couldn't be. Her breath hitched though. The thought of his palm slapping against her bare bottom made her long for things she needed to tamp down and ignore.

"Baby girl, I'm going to count to three, and then I'm going to take the decision out of your hands."

Baby girl? There was something far more intimate in those words than when he'd called her Little girl. Or maybe it was his tone. Either way, her nipples were so hard he had to notice them.

"One…"

She turned around, tugged the stairwell door open, and raced toward the steps before taking them two at a time. Half of her hoped she might escape him if she moved fast enough. The other half of her secretly hoped he would catch up to her, grab her around the waist, and make good on his threat. Would he?

She was wheezing by the time she reached the top floor. She knew better than to run up three flights of stairs. It had been a stupid move. She hoped he wouldn't notice as she burst into the hallway.

She immediately sensed Atlas at her back. The asshole wasn't even winded. But that wasn't the worst part. Her super was standing in the hallway too, leaning casually against her door.

"Jack..."

He smirked as he righted himself. "That's my name. Now, where's my money?"

"Who the fuck are you?" Atlas asked, or more like demanded in a voice that could be heard by everyone on the floor through the thin walls.

Jack didn't even flinch. He was at least six inches shorter than Atlas with a beer gut, long, greasy, thinning hair, and a silver tooth right in front. And yet, he didn't seem the least bit bothered by Atlas's presence. "Jack Turner. Apartment manager. She hasn't paid her rent." Jack kept his gaze on Carlee. "For two months," he added. He crossed his arms over his dirty T-shirt and planted his feet wide. "Last chance, Carlee. I need at least half what you owe me or you're not staying here another night."

A low wheezing sound escaped her lips when she tried to draw in a breath. *Shit. Dammit.*

"Where's your inhaler, Baby girl?" Atlas asked as he rounded in front of her, blocking her view of Jack. He set his hands on her shoulders and glanced at her purse. "In there?"

She shook her head and tried to slow her breathing. "Don't have one," she muttered. She really needed to calm her racing heart and concentrate on inhaling slowly and deeply.

"Why the fuck not? Is there one in your apartment?"

She was surprised he remembered she had asthma. She

shook her head again and leaned over, placing her hands on her knees. She hadn't had an inhaler in months. Nor had she taken a risk like running up the stairs. It had been a stupid move.

"Keys." He reached for her purse and lifted it up to rummage through it.

She couldn't even stop him. She didn't care.

Eventually he found her key ring and turned around. "Out of the way, Jack."

"Not a chance. She either pays what she owes me or she's out."

"You don't want to fuck with me, Jack. Step aside."

Carlee was secretly kind of grateful for the way Atlas was taking charge. Already her breathing was getting more under control.

Atlas reached around Jack and unlocked the door.

"You can't do that," Jack shouted. "I have the right to evict her. She's had dozens of warnings. She knew today was the final deadline."

Carlee righted herself, taking a deep oxygenated breath.

A thick vein was raised on Jack's forehead.

Atlas opened the door, flipped on the light, and then stood for several seconds staring into Carlee's apartment.

She cringed.

Finally, Atlas turned around in the open doorway and looked at Jack. "Tell you what, Jack." He pulled out his wallet and opened it.

Carlee nearly died, and she certainly would have argued if she'd had the ability to speak yet.

Atlas set a few hundreds in Jack's open palm.

"That's not even close to what she owes me."

"Is it enough to get you to go away for ten minutes?"

Jack sighed. "What for?"

"So Carlee can grab whatever's in here that's important to her. Ten minutes and we're out of here."

Carlee gasped.

Jack turned toward her, eyes narrowed. "Ten minutes, Carlee. You better be gone when I get back, or I'm calling the cops."

"You're not calling the fucking cops, Jack," Atlas argued. "If you do, I'll call the city in the morning and list all the violations I can see inside this apartment with my naked eye without even stepping inside."

Carlee thought she was going to faint.

Jack scowled. "Fine. Ten minutes." He turned around and stomped toward the stairs.

Atlas reached for Carlee's arm and gently pulled her inside. He closed the door, guided her toward her mattress, and pointed at it. "Sit."

She looked up at him. "What are you doing, Atlas?" she managed to murmur. It was surprising she was able to breathe at all considering how stressed she was.

"Getting you the fuck out of this dump."

"You can't do that." Her voice rose. She did, however, lower to sit on the shitty mattress on the floor. "I need this apartment."

"Baby girl, no one alive needs this apartment. It's not even an apartment. More like one room."

"It's a studio," she argued unnecessarily. She started trembling as she looked around.

"This is a shitty neighborhood that's completely unsafe. How long have you been living here in squalor?" He held up a hand. "Never mind. Don't answer that. We don't have time. I'm going to grab whatever looks important and get you the fuck out of here."

"I don't have anywhere else to go," she retorted.

"The hell you don't." His voice rose again. "And you have a lot of fucking explaining to do, Baby girl. When we get back to the club."

She shook her head, feeling the blood drain from her face. "I'm not going to the MC, Atlas."

He ignored her as he turned toward her tiny closet and opened it. A moment later, he had a duffle bag in his hand. He set it on the mattress and aimed for her dresser next.

She winced as he opened one drawer after another. There weren't many clothes in them.

"Where are your clothes, Carlee?" His voice was strained.

She pointed at the dirty clothes basket in the corner.

He ran a hand over his face, snagged the duffle, and set it next to the basket before dumping the contents inside.

Carlee was mortified as her dirty underwear and bras and threadbare clothes tumbled into the duffle.

"What else, Baby girl?" he asked in a calmer voice. He came to her, squatted in front of her, and cupped her face with both hands. "What do you need from this apartment?"

Tears threatened to fall down her cheeks. This was the shittiest day of her life. First her car broke down, and now she was fully humiliated to have the only man she'd ever lusted after finding out she was broke and being evicted. It was mortifying.

Atlas slid his thumbs to her cheeks and wiped away the moisture. "I'm sorry for being so gruff. I'm frustrated. I want to know what's going on with you. But we don't have time. I'd rather get out of here before your shitty super returns."

She glanced around and then shoved him aside, climbed to her feet, and headed for the bathroom. After stuffing her meager makeup and hair things into a small zippered pouch, she handed it to Atlas who was hovering in the doorway.

She reached under the far corner of her mattress next and felt around until her fingers hit the small pouch where she kept the few pieces of jewelry she owned. When she held it out, Atlas tucked it in his pocket.

Carlee turned in a slow circle. How fucking pitiful was she?

There was nothing in the tiny kitchen area she needed or wanted. The only item she wished she'd had that had been a casualty of her breakup would have been her vibrator. She'd needed it. And because it was lost to her and she didn't have the money to buy another one, she hadn't had an orgasm in months.

"Carlee?"

"There's nothing else," she whispered, humiliation making her face heat.

"Okay, Baby girl." He picked up her cardigan from the foot of the bed and held it up. "Arms."

She let him help her into it as if she were a child. And fuck if it didn't feel nice to have someone fucking take care of her for a change.

He added her grocery sack to the duffle and zipped it up before slinging it over his shoulder. Finally, he took her hand. "Let's go."

Carlee tucked her tail between her legs and let him lead her out of the apartment. It wasn't until they stepped out into the cool night air that she hesitated. She looked up at him from next to his bike. "I can't go to the club, Atlas."

"Yes, you can. Whatever's going on with you, you're going to explain it to me when we get there."

She shook her head. "No, really. I can't." She wouldn't. She didn't want to.

He glanced at his watch. "It's late. No one will even see us arrive. You'll stay in my room in the clubhouse tonight. But first, we're going to stop at an all-night pharmacy and get you an inhaler."

She drew in a sharp breath. More tears fell. "There's one already there. I haven't picked it up because I can't afford it, Atlas."

"I can."

She shook her head. "I can't let you do that."

He stepped closer to her and cupped her face. "You *will* let me do it, Baby girl. You're going to let me do a lot of things." He lifted a brow.

Her mouth fell open at the multiple implications. Fifteen minutes ago, she'd hoped to rush into her apartment building and never see Atlas again. Now he was demanding to take her back to the MC. The last place she wanted to go.

He wasn't taking no for an answer though, and she was too tired to argue with him right now. Hopefully the cool air on her face would help her clear her mind so that by the time they got to the MC, she could put her foot down and reassert herself.

But first she had to survive another trip on Atlas's bike with her arms around his strong body and his scent in her nose.

Such a hardship.

CHAPTER
THREE

Atlas was tense as he parked his bike behind the clubhouse, slid off the side, and lifted Carlee off behind him. She had a lot of talking to do, but he suspected it was going to be like pulling teeth to get her to open up. In addition, she was exhausted. She'd leaned into him hard between the pharmacy and the MC.

After adjusting her duffle bag on his shoulder, he removed her helmet and stowed it on the seat. "Let's get you inside."

She glanced around and rubbed her arms. "I'm not welcome here, Atlas," she informed him.

He jerked his attention to her face. "Why the hell not?" Now he was even more concerned about her. He couldn't imagine a scenario in which Carlee Deveraux wouldn't be welcome at the MC.

She tipped her head back. "Atlas, I don't want to talk about this. I'm exhausted. I have to be at work early in the morning. I don't have a car, and now I don't have an apartment either." Tears slid down her cheeks, and she swiped at them before he could do so himself.

"Come on." He took her hand. In fact, he threaded their fingers together and tugged her toward the back entrance to the club. It was a weeknight and late, so few people would be up in the main area, but if he snuck her in through the back, he could get her into his room without anyone noticing.

He had no idea why this was necessary, but he'd take her word for it and get answers later.

Luckily, no one was in the hallway when he opened the door, and he had her in his private room in less than a minute. "Sit," he ordered, pointing at the bed.

She looked around as she lowered herself onto the mattress. "I've never seen a room this clean and tidy inside the club," she muttered.

He chuckled. "I just got here today. My dad probably had ten people get this room ready for me. I'm sure he thinks I'll stay in town if he sweetens the deal with a nice room, clean sheets, vacuumed floors, and a bleached bathroom. I'm surprised he didn't insist I take an apartment."

"Will you?" she asked, eyes wide.

"No." He squatted down in front of her and set his hands on the mattress on either side of her hips. He wanted to touch her. Hell, he wanted to do a lot more than touch her, but he shouldn't. "I'm here for one month to help out the club. Apparently you need some help too."

She shook her head. Her defiant side was frustrating but kind of cute at the same time. "I was doing just fine until you showed up."

He lifted both brows. "Is that so? It didn't look like you were doing fine to me. Your car was broken down on the side of the road, and you wouldn't have been able to retrieve anything from your apartment before you were evicted if I hadn't been there."

She rolled her eyes. "We aren't all perfect like you, Atlas. In real life, people have financial difficulties." She glanced at the clock on the nightstand. "Shit."

He looked too. It was almost midnight. "What time do you need to be at work?"

"Five-thirty."

He stiffened. "In the morning?"

"Yes." She fisted her hands on her lap and glared at him. "Now you have a problem with my working hours too?"

He shook his head. "No. Sorry. I was just surprised. Where do you work?"

"At the diner on the west side of town."

"Then I'll set an alarm for four-thirty. Does that give you enough time?"

"Enough time for what? Shit." She slapped a palm over her forehead. "I don't have a car."

He tried not to chuckle. She was really tired if she didn't remember that fact.

"I'll take you. We'll leave at five-ten." He shoved off the bed and rose to his feet before pointing toward the attached bathroom. "Go use the potty, Baby girl. Brush your teeth. I bet there's a spare toothbrush in one of the drawers."

Her breath hitched, and she stared at him for a few seconds before complying.

He watched her cute ass as she stepped into the bathroom and shut the door. He hadn't even unpacked his suitcase yet, so he tipped it onto the floor, opened it up, and grabbed a T-shirt. It didn't appear Carlee had even one clean article of clothing.

Atlas grabbed her duffle and opened it to tug out the grocery sack and her toiletry bag. He set her stuffed hamster and the bear he'd given her on the pillow and the duffle back by the door. He'd do a load of her laundry while she slept.

After knocking on the bathroom door, he called out, "Can I come in?"

"Yes."

When he opened the door, he found her sticking the toothbrush in the holder. He set her toiletry bag on the counter. "I wasn't sure if you needed anything from here." He held up his

T-shirt. "Put this on and hand me your clothes. I'm going to start a load of laundry for you."

She pursed her lips, not moving. Finally, she snagged the T-shirt. "I don't like this, Atlas."

"You don't like what, Baby girl?"

"You helping me. You treating me like you're my Daddy."

"Seems like you're kind of in need of a Daddy, Carlee," he pointed out.

She shook her head. "I don't want another Daddy. I'm fine on my own. Besides, you said yourself you're leaving in a month."

He tipped her chin back and looked into her eyes, honing in on the first thing she'd said. "*Another* Daddy? Did you have a Daddy before, Baby girl?"

She rolled her naughty eyes. "We're not discussing this."

"Oh, we are, but not tonight. You need to sleep every moment you can between now and four-thirty. I don't like the idea of you going to work on so little sleep. Why were you out so late if you have to work tomorrow morning so early?"

Her eyes widened. "Don't you dare judge me, Atlas Monroe."

He drew in a deep breath. "There are about a dozen reasons why I should take you over my knees right now and spank your naughty bottom. And don't think you're going to get out of it either. I'm not going to do so right now because you need to sleep. Nor am I going to pull information out of you for the same reason. But after I pick you back up from work tomorrow, we're going to talk, Little girl. That talk is going to include a firm spanking. If you argue with me about it, I'll double the spanking. Have I made myself clear?"

She glared at him. "Crystal clear, *Daddy*." She couldn't have added that last word with any more sass if she'd tried.

He couldn't decide whether to laugh or growl. He did neither. "Do you want to shower now or in the morning?"

She glanced at the glass shower enclosure. "Now. I…"

"You what?" he asked when she hesitated.

"I'm not a morning person," she murmured.

"Well, lucky for you, four-thirty is not morning. Not even for me. That's still the middle of the night." He grinned before releasing her chin to turn around, open the glass door, and twist the knob so the water came on. "Clothes off," he ordered.

When he turned around, he found her hands on her hips, her eyes glaring at him. "I'm not getting naked in front of you, Atlas."

"I've seen naked Little girls before, sassy pants."

She gasped, her mouth dropping open. "What did you just call me?"

"Sassy pants. If the shoe fits..." He moved toward the door, pulled it open, and stepped into the bedroom. What he did not do was shut the door. He didn't like the idea of even turning away from her, but he would. Just this once.

He stood in the doorway, facing out. "I'll give you about fifteen seconds to remove your clothes and set them in my hand. If you don't comply, miss sassy pants, I'll turn around and take those clothes off myself. Your choice."

He grinned as he heard her shoes hit the floor followed by the zipper of her jeans. In ten seconds flat, she set the bundle of clothes in his hand, shoved him forward, and slammed the door.

He chuckled as he headed for the duffle bag to add today's clothes. After that, he lifted the duffle and stepped into the hall. The path to the laundry room was vacant, thank God. He still didn't have a single indication as to why Carlee didn't want to be at the MC, but he now suspected it had something to do with the fact that she'd had a Daddy at some point.

He hurried to the laundry room, dumped her clothes into the washer, added detergent, and started the machine. When he turned around, he flinched. "Hey, Remi. I wondered when you were going to hunt me down." He tried to sound casual as he spoke to his sister.

He hadn't seen her yet since his arrival. Hell, he hadn't seen many people at all yet. He'd dropped his suitcase in his temporary assigned room, gone in search of his bike, and taken off for a ride. It had been a long time since he'd felt the wind against his face and arms, the exhilaration of riding.

That's how he'd ended up out so late and accidentally stumbled upon Carlee. Had it been fate?

"You're already doing laundry?" Remi teased.

Her style hadn't changed a bit in recent years. It still included black clothes, dark makeup, and dark hair. When she turned her head, however, he noticed a hot pink bow. That was new. He forced himself not to smirk. He wondered if Kade had anything to do with the flash of pink.

She cocked a hip out. "You just got here. That's so unlike you. I would have expected you to arrive with your shirts organized on hangers by color and your underwear folded in your suitcase."

He narrowed his gaze and crossed his arms. No way was he going to tell her what had gone into the washer. "Ha ha." He dropped his arms and approached her, backing her out of the laundry room. "What are you doing here in the middle of the night? I thought you and Kade were living at his house."

She shrugged. "Kade had some shit to do. I'm just hanging out here waiting for him. Come have a drink with me. We need to catch up."

"Can't." He nodded toward the hall of rooms. "Rain check?"

She stood rooted in the hallway. "What the fuck, Atlas?" A slow grin spread across her face. "Don't tell me you already have a woman in your room."

"Do you use that kind of language with Kade?" he said to redirect the conversation.

"Yep. When I want my ass paddled." She twirled a lock of her hair. "Now answer my question. Who is she?"

"You have an overactive imagination, little sister. I need sleep. Come find me tomorrow." He turned to head down the hallway in the direction of his room. He wouldn't ordinarily be so curt with his sister. Never. But for some reason, Carlee didn't want anyone to know she was here, so he'd respect that wish, for now.

"You're a shitty liar, Atlas," Remi called after him. "But I'll let it slide for now. Expect to play twenty questions tomorrow though."

He ignored her and stepped back into his room, locking the door behind him. Good timing too because the shower was no longer running and the bathroom door opened.

All the breath left his lungs as Carlee stepped into the room. Her hair was still in the pigtails, but the ends were damp. His T-shirt was huge on her. It came down to almost her knees. It didn't hide her pert breasts or her tight little nipples though. And his cock grew hard because he knew she wasn't wearing panties underneath.

She fidgeted her hands in front of her and glanced at the bed. "We're not sleeping together, Atlas."

He swiped his hand down his face and took a deep breath. Everything with this Little girl was going to be a battle apparently. After crossing the room, he pulled back the covers. "Get in."

She didn't move.

He looked at her. "Carlee Marie, do I need to count to three again tonight, sassy pants? It's late, but if you'll sleep better after a bare-bottom spanking, I'll be happy to oblige."

She rushed over and climbed onto the bed, trying hard to keep his shirt under her bottom. Probably for the best. If he got a look at her sweet little pussy, he would probably drop to his knees. There was no doubt the only thing on his mind was suddenly the thought of sucking her sweet juices until she cried out her release.

Shaking the thought from his mind, he pulled the covers

over her, reached for her hamster stuffie, and tucked it in her arms. The new bear sat near her head.

She was stiff and wide-eyed.

He sat on the edge of the bed. "Here's the thing. You have two choices. I can sleep on top of the covers on the other side of the bed or I can go out into the main room and find a couch to sleep on."

She opened her mouth, but he stopped her with a finger to her lips. "There's a glitch in option number two. I had fully intended to go sleep out there, but I ran into my sister after I put your clothes in the washer. When I begged her off, she decided I must have a woman in my room."

Carlee gasped. Her eyes were even wider with panic.

Atlas's blood pressure picked up. Whatever the fuck was up with her was pissing him off, especially if it involved Remi. Carlee and Remi had been best friends since kindergarten.

He lifted a brow. "If you really don't think you can trust me to maintain your virtue, I could sleep on the floor."

She rolled her eyes. "My virtue? Ha." She glanced at the other side of the bed. "Fine. But keep your hands on your side of the bed."

"What about my legs?" he teased.

She groaned as she rolled onto her side, faced her side of the mattress, and curled into a ball, hugging the hamster against her chest. When the bear rolled into her face, she tugged him under the covers too.

"What's his name?" Atlas asked, patting the worn hamster with his hand.

"Hammie," she whispered. "I was two when I got him. I didn't know he needed a better name."

Atlas's heartstrings tugged hard. There were a lot of facets to this Little girl in his bed. She could be pigheaded and fierce. She could be teary and scared. She could also be soft and so very Little. He leaned over and kissed her temple. "I think Hammie is a fine name. I won't forget it."

She didn't respond.

"Sleep, Baby girl. I'll go move your laundry to the dryer in a bit and wake you up on time to go to work."

She bit her lip and gave a slight nod without looking at him.

For several minutes he remained sitting on the edge of the bed, rubbing her back, helping her settle. He told himself he didn't want to move until she was deep asleep as if he was calming her. But the truth was he didn't want to move ever. He was selfish. He wanted to stay right here and stare at her as her features relaxed in sleep.

Who was he kidding? He wanted more. He wanted to take care of her, Daddy her, hold her, find out what the fuck was going on with her and fix it. The instinct was visceral. He couldn't shake it.

He'd been gone for ten years, only visiting occasionally on holidays. He'd left for college even before that, convinced he wanted to get out of this small town, get a degree, and enter the white-collar workforce.

Atlas loved his job. Most of the time. But it was lonely too. He worked long hours in an office building. He rarely dated, and when he did, it never amounted to anything. He knew why. It didn't take a rocket scientist for him to know he was a Daddy.

He'd been born into an MC club comprised mostly of Daddies. It was what he knew. It was in his blood. No matter how long he was away, he was still a Daddy at heart. And Little girls did not frequent the places he went.

She was asleep now. He wanted to climb behind her and spoon her body against his. He wanted to strip to his boxers, get under the covers, and wrap his arms and legs around her.

He'd promised her he wouldn't touch her though. He understood where she was coming from. After all, he'd made it clear he was not staying in town. It would be cruel to Daddy her and walk away. To both of them.

He was seeing Carlee in a whole new light tonight. She wasn't the teenager he remembered from his graduation party. She was a grown woman. A very sexy, sassy, adorable, stubborn grown woman. One with a pile of problems that needed addressing.

There was no way he could promise her a future, but he'd be damned if he'd turn his back on her this month. He fully intended to get all up in her business and help her get her life back on track.

Glancing at the clock, he realized it was already time to move her laundry. He rose to his feet, careful not to disturb her, and slipped from the room, turning off the overhead light as he went.

The bathroom light was still on. She wouldn't be confused if she woke up scared. Plus, he didn't intend to be gone more than a few minutes.

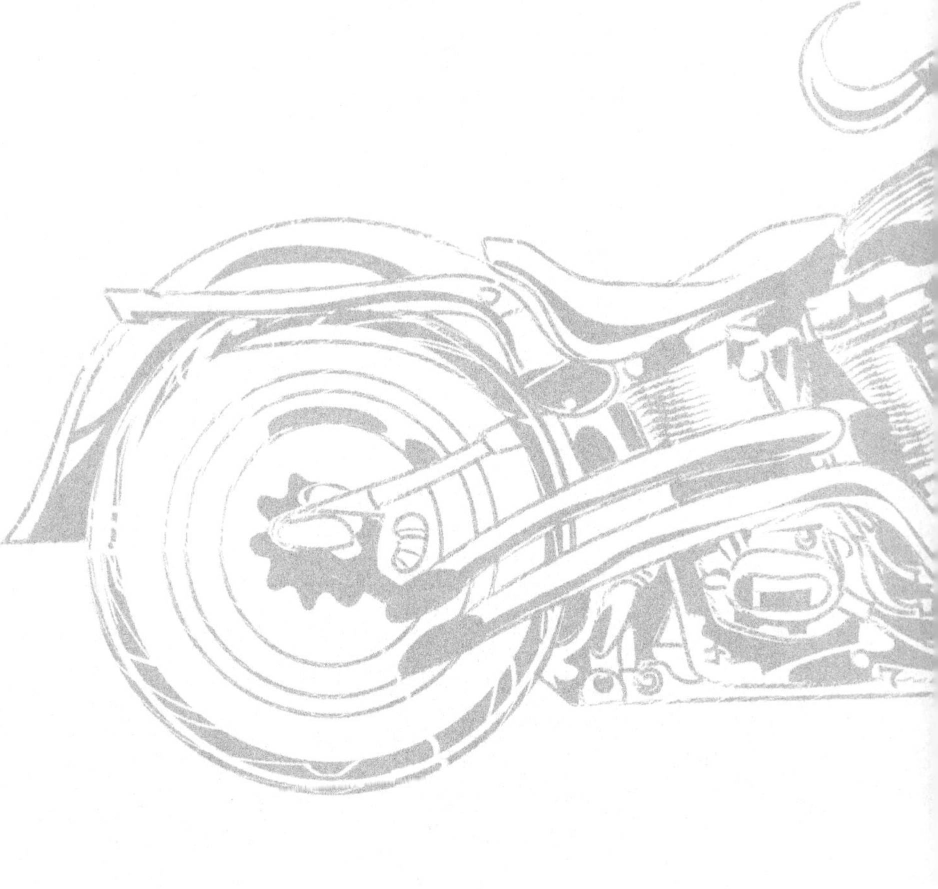

CHAPTER
FOUR

"Hey, Baby girl..."

Carlee groaned at the sound of the deep voice dragging her from sleep. She knew it wasn't real. No one was in her apartment talking to her. No one had *ever* been in her apartment, let alone a Daddy.

She snuggled in deeper. It couldn't be morning yet, and her alarm wasn't going off, so...

A hand smoothed the hair away from her cheek before warm lips kissed her temple. "Time to get up, Little one."

She held her breath. What a weird dream.

"My little sassy pants meant it when she said she's not a morning person, didn't she?"

Carlee knew that voice. She yanked her eyes open to find Atlas sitting on the edge of her bed, smiling down at her. No, not her bed. *His* bed. In the clubhouse.

Shit. She pushed to sitting and looked around, finding the clock. Four-thirty. At least she wasn't late.

"If I make you something to eat, I bet you can snooze for ten more minutes and still have plenty of time," he suggested.

She met his gaze. "I don't eat before work."

He frowned. "That's not healthy. Little girls need to eat in the morning."

"It's hardly morning," she pointed out. "And I eat at the diner." She shifted her attention to the piles of clothes folded and stacked on top of the dresser. "Did you sleep at all?" she asked, feeling embarrassed to realize he'd stayed up washing and drying her clothes and then folding them. Including her panties and bras.

Her face heated at the thought of him handling her intimates.

"A few hours. I'll sleep later today." He tugged the covers back as he stood. "Go potty, wash your face, and brush your teeth."

She bit her lip as he stepped toward her piles of clothes. "What do you wear to work, Baby girl?"

Every time he called her that, her heart seized. She wasn't sure if she hated it or loved it. She wished she could be his Baby girl, but since she couldn't, she'd rather he didn't call her that. It sent shivers down her arms and legs.

When he turned toward her, brow lifted, she scrambled out of bed, shaking off the way he affected her.

He pointed at the clothes.

"Oh, uh, whatever I want. I wear an apron when I get there. Just jeans and a T-shirt." She stood frozen in her spot as she watched him choose clothes for her as if he were really her Daddy and in charge of her outfits.

He pulled out a pair of jeans, a hot-pink T-shirt, a pair of white cotton panties, and a white bra. When he turned around to hand them to her, she couldn't breathe.

Did he have any idea how hard he was dominating her? Maybe he dominated everyone like this. Maybe it came second nature to him.

"Are you going to do as you're told, Baby girl? Or do you need me to come into the bathroom with you and supervise?"

Her breath hitched. He wasn't kidding. No way in hell was

she going to let him go that far. No matter how tempting it was. She could not fall for him. No. Just no. No no no no. If she did, he would break her heart.

She snatched the clothes from his hands and hurried past him, not breathing until she had shut the door and leaned against it. She was trembling from head to toe as her mind replayed his words.

"Are you going to do as you're told, Baby girl? Or do you need me to come into the bathroom with you and supervise?"

No one had ever Daddied her like that. Never. She'd longed for someone to do so, but she'd never met the right Daddy. Except Atlas, of course. She'd always imagined him as a firm, commanding Daddy, but she'd never witnessed it firsthand.

She couldn't stand here all day. If she didn't hurry, he was liable to open the bathroom door before she had her clothes on. That would be mortifying. More mortifying than the thought of him folding her panties.

She set the bundle on the vanity before quickly using the toilet, brushing her teeth, and washing her face. She pulled his T-shirt over her head and set it aside before hurrying to put her clothes on.

It was easier to breathe once she had that much done. At least if the overbearing Daddy came barging into the bathroom now, she would be covered.

Her next task was going to take some time. Her hair. It was a tangled mess, still up in the pigtails she'd worn yesterday. After finding her brush, she removed one of the bands, worked through all the tangles, and put the mess of curls up in a little bun in the place of yesterday's pigtail.

She repeated the process on the other side before rummaging for her mascara and lip gloss. She rarely wore more makeup than that. For one thing, she couldn't afford it. For another thing, she just didn't care. Remi had tried to help her learn to put eyeshadow, eyeliner, and rouge on several times in their teens, but Carlee had never cared enough to do it herself.

When she stepped out of the bathroom, she found Atlas sitting on the bed. He had her shoes and socks in his hands. He smiled at her. "Come sit. Let's get your shoes on."

"I can do it myself," she insisted as she strode toward him, feeling defiant. Or maybe just vulnerable. She needed him to stop Daddying her. She was going to get hurt.

"I'm sure you can, but it seems to me you've been doing far too much for a long time. Why don't you relax and let me take care of you?"

Because you're going to break my heart. You probably already have.

Carlee shuffled closer, fully intent on snatching the shoes and socks from his hands, but she couldn't do it. She was too tired to argue, and it felt so damn good having someone take care of her.

Instead, she let him lift her by the waist, set her in the middle of the bed, and put her shoes and socks on. She bit her bottom lip and held her breath the entire time, watching his big hands and the ripple of muscles across his shoulders. She wanted to run her hands through his thick brown hair. She wanted to feel his short beard rubbing against her... *Stop it!*

She needed to get a grip on herself. She turned her face away and drew in a deep breath. That was a horrible idea because it was filled with his scent. He'd only arrived yesterday, but already this room smelled like him. Like man. Like a Daddy. Like *her* Daddy.

"There," he declared when he was finished. He rose to standing, lifted her off the bed, set her on her feet, and grabbed her cardigan from the back of the desk chair. "Arms, Baby girl."

She let him put the sweater on her.

He picked up a helmet from the desk next.

"Where did you get that?" she asked.

"It wasn't hard. There are plenty of helmets in the garage to fit all sizes. After all, it's a motorcycle club," he joked. "Ready?"

She nodded, hoping once again no one would be up and see her sneaking out of the clubhouse. She was grateful he wasn't making light of her desire to hide as he opened the door and looked up and down the hall before ushering her out and then out the back door once again too.

He put the helmet on her and buckled it before securing his own, tossing a muscular leg over the seat, and grabbing her arm to help her get on behind him. He powered up the bike and took off quickly, bless him.

She breathed easier after they left the compound and got on the open road. She also flattened her front to his back and held on tight around his waist, wanting to soak up every moment of this contact with him. She was going to get burned badly in the end, but for now, she only cared about enjoying the moment.

Less than fifteen minutes later, Atlas pulled up to the diner, shut off the bike, and helped her down.

"Thank you," she murmured. She had no idea how she was going to repay him for his help, but then again, she also knew he would be insulted and probably make good on his threat of spanking her if she suggested such a thing.

He climbed off the bike next. "Let's get you inside."

She glanced up at him. "You don't need to come in." She looked toward the diner. There weren't many customers inside yet, but they would start arriving soon. There was an early morning rush of older folks who liked to eat out for breakfast.

Atlas gave her his no-nonsense look, set a hand on her back, and ushered her toward the diner.

Carlee really didn't want him to come inside. Her boss was a dick. He would inevitably yell at her as soon as she came through the door, and Atlas would cause a scene.

There was no arguing with Atlas though, so she prayed

Marv would be in a good mood today, though she couldn't remember the last time that had happened.

Atlas opened the front door, ushered her in front of him, and then followed her into the diner. He stayed on her heels as she headed for the back room where she would pick up her apron and clock in.

As she passed her coworker Eden, the woman lifted her brows, glancing over Carlee's shoulder at the enormous man behind her. "Good morning, Carlee."

Carlee sighed, knowing she was eventually going to have to explain Atlas's hovering presence, but not now.

When Carlee glanced at him, thinking to tell him he should go now, she found a gruff expression that had her slamming her mouth shut. *Fuck.* She might not know Atlas very well after his ten-year absence, but she knew most of the members of the MC. Ninety percent of them would not leave her here without meeting her boss first and ensuring she was okay.

Atlas might not have been in town often for a decade, but apparently that trait had not worn off. He was on her heels, determined to follow her.

"You're late." The growly voice made Carlee jump as she entered the small employee room where Marv sat at his desk with his back to her. And Atlas.

"Sorry, sir," she murmured.

"I thought you told me you were supposed to be here at five-thirty. It's only five-fifteen," Atlas said.

Carlee cringed as she grabbed an apron.

Marv spun around on his swivel chair, scowling. "Who the fuck are you?"

"A friend of Carlee's. What time was she supposed to clock in today?" Atlas looked even larger than usual with his feet planted and his hands on his hips. He filled the entire doorframe.

Marv turned his narrowed gaze on Carlee. "What the hell are you doing bringing someone to the back room?" He shoved to his feet, obviously trying to look as large and intimidating as Atlas. And failing miserably. He was several inches shorter, not in good physical shape, and kind of greasy.

"He's just dropping me off, and I'm not late," she defended, though she usually made a point of ignoring the first thing he said to her nearly every day.

He grunted. "You better not be dragging your ass today. It's going to be busy. You were so lazy last night I should dock your pay."

Atlas jerked his attention to Carlee. "You were working last night?"

She pursed her lips.

"Who the fuck are you, anyway?" Marv growled. "Get out of my diner before I dock her pay for real."

Atlas took another step into the back room instead of retreating.

Carlee's heart was racing. This was not going to go well.

Atlas ignored Marv's order. "What time did she get off last night?"

"She closed. How is this any of your business?" Marv hiked up his slouching jeans.

Atlas leaned in closer, baring his teeth. "What time do you close?"

"Ten o'clock, asshole." Marv pointed at Carlee. "Tell your boyfriend to get the fuck out."

"He's not my boyfriend," she murmured for some odd reason.

Atlas ignored both of them and took yet another step closer. "What time did she leave the diner?"

"What the fuck is wrong with you, asshole?" Marv retorted.

"What time did she leave the diner?" Atlas repeated, keeping his voice even.

Marv tossed his arms in the air. "I don't fucking know. Eleven probably."

"Do you always schedule your employees to be back at work six and a half hours later, knowing they can't possibly get enough sleep, and then yell at them when they are fifteen minutes early?"

Shit. Shit shit shit.

Marv's face turned red. "Just the lazy ones who are barely worth keeping on my payroll."

Tears stung Carlee's eyes. She was not lazy. She'd never been lazy in her life. She worked her ass off for so little pay she couldn't make rent. The tips in this diner were awful. But she needed this job. And Atlas was going to get her fired.

Atlas pulled in a long breath and narrowed his gaze on Marv. He didn't glance at Carlee as he said, "Take that apron off, Carlee. You're not staying here."

She nearly jumped out of her skin. *No no no no no no.* Oh no he did not. She didn't move to do his bidding. "You should go," she said, working hard to hold back the tears. What was wrong with him?

"Yep. We're going to leave just as soon as this asshole cuts your last check including everything he owes you up until eleven p.m. last night." He still didn't glance at her.

"Atlas..." All the blood ran from her face. He was being an overbearing dick. What right did he have to swoop into town and take over her life? He was ruining everything, and he wasn't even fucking staying.

Atlas calmly continued, staring daggers at Marv. "Turn around and cut her a check right now."

Marv looked like his head was going to explode. "Who the fuck do you think you are, ordering me around? What the hell am I supposed to do without my waitress this morning?"

"According to you she wasn't worth having on staff anyway."

Carlee wanted to punch Atlas in the stomach, and she would have if she could have moved. Instead, she was frozen to her spot. Stuck. Rooted. Still wearing the apron. This could not be happening.

Atlas spoke again. "I've known Carlee since she was five years old. I know she is hard-working and dedicated to everything she does, which means you're a bully and a liar. I don't give a fuck what you do for a waitress this morning or this afternoon or tonight or tomorrow. But you're going to do it without Carlee. Maybe you should go out front and wait tables yourself for a few days until you learn to appreciate your staff and treat them better. If this is how you treat everyone who works for you, it's a wonder you're able to keep anyone working for you at all. Now. Turn. The fuck. Around. And cut. Carlee. A check."

Carlee jumped in her spot again at his tone.

Several seconds passed in a stare down.

"I don't have to do fuck, asshole," Marv stated. "If she wants to quit, she can fucking leave without pay."

Atlas pulled out his phone.

"Who the fuck are you calling?" Marv asked, his face growing redder.

"The cops in about five seconds."

Marv's scowl deepened and he fisted his hands before he finally turned around, dropped into his chair, and snagged his checkbook from the drawer.

Carlee couldn't move.

Atlas turned toward her finally and silently untied the apron, lifted it over her head, and set it back on the stack. "Do you have any belongings here?" he asked calmly as if he were inquiring about the weather.

She stared at him, swallowing hard, barely holding back tears. She didn't even shake her head. She was a statue. Her ears were ringing. She needed a redo of the past…six hours. Or maybe she should go back a bit before that and walk away from her car faster so he couldn't find her on the side of the road at all.

Atlas picked up her purse and lowered it over her head so it crossed her body. When he was finished, he turned back around and took the check from Marv before tucking it deep into her purse and snapping the top shut. "Let's go."

Carlee's feet wouldn't move. She literally couldn't get the message to them.

Atlas physically turned her to face the door, set a hand on her back, and guided her back through the diner.

"Carlee?" Eden reached out and touched her arm as she passed. She stepped closer and whispered in her ear, "You okay?"

Carlee was barely holding back tears as she pursed her lips. She wondered how loud that interaction had been, but a glance around at everyone told her they had all heard every single word.

Eden looked concerned, and she was shaking, probably worried about how this day was going to go.

Carlee swiped at the tears gathering in her eyes. "I'm sorry," she apologized.

"No need to be sorry." Eden glanced up at the hovering hulk behind Carlee again with his hand possessively on her back.

Carlee wanted to slap it away and tell him to go fuck himself, but she didn't want to draw more attention to herself. Everyone in the diner was staring at her. Their expressions were sympathetic though. Thank God.

"You're so lucky," Eden whispered. "I wish I had a man who would waltz in here and stick up for me like that."

Carlee didn't feel lucky. She felt like her life was crumbling around her. She'd lost her car, her apartment, and her job since Atlas had shown up in her life last night. Had that been six hours ago?

She was furious, her anger growing by the second.

Eden didn't understand though. She smiled and gave Carlee a quick hug. "Guess I better get to work. It's going to be a long morning around here. Good luck. Call me sometime."

Carlee nodded, gritting her teeth before she continued out the front door. She vaguely heard Marv behind her shouting at her not to fucking come crawling back to him after her high-handed boyfriend got tired of her and dumped her lazy ass.

When they stepped outside, the cool air shook Carlee from her nearly catatonic state. It was still dark, but the sun would be peeking over the horizon soon.

Fury consumed her. She jerked away from Atlas's touch and stomped toward the road.

"Carlee? Where are you going?"

She tossed a middle finger over her shoulder, hugged her sweater around her, and kept walking as fast as her short legs could carry her.

She could hear Atlas's boots on the pavement as he jogged to catch up with her, and then he rounded in front of her and grabbed her biceps. "What are you doing?"

"Leaving," she shouted. "Let go of me and get out of my way."

"Carlee… Be reasonable. It's dark and cold out, and where are you going to go?"

"I don't have a fucking clue, Atlas. You've turned my fucking life upside down in six hours. Last night I had a car, and apartment, and a job. Suddenly, I have none of those things. So get out of my fucking way. I need to think, and I can't do that with you all up in my face."

He shook his head. "I'm not going to leave you here, Little girl. Get back on my bike. I'll take you back to the MC. We can discuss your situation there."

"No. You think you can fix this? You can't. We aren't all perfect like you, Atlas. Not everyone went to college and got a degree and can just walk away from a job or an apartment or a shitty car."

He drew in a breath, his brow furrowed. "You can't blame

me for the fact that your car is a piece of shit. Nor can you blame me for the fact that you got evicted. The job is on me, but that guy was a fucking dick. You can't work for someone who treats you like shit, Carlee."

She gasped. "Welcome to the real world, Atlas. We work for dicks so we can pay for tow trucks and get Band-Aids put on our vehicles so they will run another month. And for your information, I would have found a way to get past Jack last night. He wouldn't have really put me out in the street. He was bluffing."

His eyes widened to saucers. "Found a way?" Finally his voice lifted. "What were you going to bargain with, Carlee?" he shouted. His grip tightened on her arms.

She gasped. The tears wouldn't hold back another moment. They fell down her face in rivers, streaking her cheeks right before she let out a sob. She jerked free of his clutch and started walking again. "Fuck you, Atlas," she shouted over her shoulder.

He came after her again. Of course. This time, he grabbed her from behind, wrapped his arms around her, and hauled her back against his front.

She tried to wiggle free, but he was much larger and stronger. She was also sobbing like a giant baby now. The kind of crying anyone for a block around could hear. Luckily it wasn't likely many people were around at five-thirty in the morning.

His lips came to her ear. "I'm sorry, Baby girl. I didn't mean it like that at all. I would never accuse you of selling your body. I was picturing that jewelry you pulled out from under your mattress or something else you might have sold to a pawn shop. I hated the idea of you parting with what few things you own that must be sentimental to pay the rent."

He reached up and wiped her tears with his thumb. "Please get on my bike," he whispered against her ear. "Please, Baby girl. Let's go back to my room and talk."

She went boneless in his arms. "Don't do that," she whimpered.

"Do what?"

"Baby girl me. It's not fair."

He gave a slight chuckle against her neck and then kissed her there, which made her toes curl and her heart race. "I apologize. Please come with me."

She liked that he was being less highhanded. Slightly less.

"I needed that job," she murmured.

"Your boss was a huge dick. Let me help you find another job, okay?"

"I'm probably blacklisted in this town. I don't have skills for anything that's available," she whined.

"I don't believe that. You just need confidence. I promise to help you figure out what you're good at and find a more suitable job with a less misogynistic boss." He gave her a squeeze. "Would you like to walk over to my bike and climb on behind me? Or would you rather I toss you over my shoulder and carry you there?"

"You wouldn't."

"Try me. I can count to three if you want. You seem to respond well to that."

She sighed, her body deflating. Her world really was upside down. She had a lot of problems. She couldn't blame him for the car problem. She probably couldn't blame him for the apartment problem either. If she'd sweet-talked Jack into letting her stay last night, it would have only been a matter of days before she came home to find her stuff in the street and the lock changed.

The job was Atlas's fault. Though he was right. Marv was a dick-faced bootyhead. She hated him. At least she didn't have to listen to him berate her condescendingly anymore.

"One..."

She flinched in his arms. "Okay. Okay."

When he released her, she let him lead her to his bike

where she climbed up behind him yet again, leaned her cheek against his back, and closed her eyes. She would pretend he was her Daddy for real and that he was going to take care of her and never leave town. She could at least pretend. That was all she had going for her right now.

CHAPTER
FIVE

The sun was barely up when Atlas once again parked his bike behind the clubhouse and led Carlee back into his room. No one saw them. Few people had been up last night when they'd arrived, and few people were up this early in the morning either.

Within minutes, they were back in his room. He settled her on his bed, removed her shoes, and leaned her against a pile of pillows. "Don't move. I'm going to find us some food. I know you have to be starving."

She grabbed Hammie and the new bear and hugged them tight, looking extremely Little as she nodded.

Atlas's chest was tight as he looked at her. She was so fucking cute. So damn sweet and perfect in every way. How had he never seen her through his Daddy lens before?

Because she was far too young to glance twice at when you last lived here.

He couldn't help himself. He leaned over, kissed her forehead, and gave her a pointed look. "You won't run away on me, right?"

She shook her head, the cute buns she'd constructed on top bouncing. "I don't have anywhere to go."

"I promise to fix that." He shoved off the mattress and headed for the kitchen. He knew he could find something quick and easy they could eat. And he was right. Bingo.

There were several boxes of frozen breakfast sandwiches in the freezer. He grabbed a sausage, egg, and cheese biscuit and popped it in the microwave before also selecting a ham, egg, and cheese croissant. She could choose. He would eat either.

He snagged a bottle of orange juice from the fridge, two plastic tumblers, and an individual carton of milk in case she preferred milk. He had no idea what this Little girl liked to eat, but it suddenly seemed imperative that he find out.

He wanted to know every single thing about her, starting with why her life was so off track and why she wasn't reaching out to the Shadowridge Guardians for help. From there he would move on to mundane things like her favorite color, movies, music. Everything. He wanted to know it all. Now. Today.

The microwave pinged, alerting him the second sandwich was done, and he balanced all the items in his arms and headed back down the hallway, grateful no one was around to question his early morning appetite.

It took a juggling act to turn the doorknob, but he managed, and let out a relieved breath when he found Carlee right where he'd left her on the bed.

She slid off the side and helped him by taking a few things from his arms and setting them on the desk. "You didn't have to do this," she murmured.

"Feed you? Yes, I did. Plus I'm running on fumes myself." He set the tumblers down first. "Milk or juice?"

She chewed on her bottom lip adorably.

"Never mind. You can have both." He opened the small carton of milk and handed it to her. "Can you drink from the carton so I can use the cup for juice, Baby girl? If you want, I can go back and look for a sippy cup. I bet they have a stash of them in the kitchen."

She lifted her gaze to his, her eyes wide, her bottom lip tucked between her teeth.

That was the moment he knew she was not just the most adorable Little on earth, but his. His Baby girl.

It hit him like a freight train, nearly knocking him off his feet. He even stumbled back a step and had to grab the back of the desk chair.

"The carton is fine," she finally whispered.

He snapped his fingers. "Darn. I forgot coffee. I'm going to need a lot of coffee. I'll grab a sippy cup while I'm getting it." He lifted her off her feet and settled her back on the bed before holding up both sandwiches. "Sausage, egg, and cheese biscuit or ham, egg, and cheese croissant?"

She leaned over them both, deliberating.

Fuck, but she was cute. So fucking cute. So goddamn fucking cute that his heart hurt. He set both sandwiches in front of her on the blankets. "You pick, or eat half of each one or both. I can always get more. There are plenty in the kitchen." He kissed her forehead again and headed back out for coffee and sippy cups.

This time he wasn't as lucky in the kitchen. If he had to run into someone though, he was grateful it was at least his dad.

"Hey, what are you doing up so early?" Rock asked.

"Long story. I can't talk about it now. I promise to come talk to you later if you'll please not ask questions now."

His dad stared at him, brow furrowed. "You okay?"

"Yep." Atlas pointed at the pot of coffee his father had made. "May I please have a cup of coffee?"

Rock stepped aside. "Of course."

Atlas grabbed a large mug from the counter, filled it, and then started opening drawers. It took four before he found what he was looking for. He grabbed two sippy cups, picked up his mug of coffee, and met his father's gaze.

Rock hadn't moved an inch. His brows were lifted to the

ceiling. His gaze was on the sippy cups in Atlas's hand. He slowly lifted it to his son's face. "You'll come find me later."

"Yes. And I know you need me to start looking at the books today. Can you trust me, please? Something has come up that's urgent. I need to take care of this first. As soon as I'm able, I'll come find you. We'll talk. You can bring me up to speed."

Rock gave a slow nod.

"And Dad…"

"I won't mention a word of this, son."

"Thank you."

Atlas turned and headed back down the hallway. He knew his father had mixed feelings about him. He had for many years. On the one hand, he was proud as fuck that his son had gotten a college degree and followed his dreams. On the other hand, he'd always wished his son would return to the fold and rejoin the MC.

Fuck. Maybe he would get his damn wish after all. For the first time in more years than Atlas could count, he found himself considering a life with the MC he'd left when he was eighteen.

He was functioning on very little sleep. Adrenaline was all that was keeping him upright. But nearly seven hours ago the sweetest Little girl ever had leaned over the back of her trunk and stolen his heart.

He'd been bulldozed by the realization just a few minutes ago in his room, but if he was honest, she'd probably burrowed her way into his heart the moment she'd turned around and he'd recognized her last night. Those cute pigtails. The tight pink T-shirt. Her body-hugging jeans. And those scuffed, worn sneakers.

He slipped back into the room to find her chewing on a huge bite of sandwich. After setting the coffee and cups on the desk, he returned to lock the bedroom door. The last thing he wanted was for his sister or another club member to barge in while he was trying to sort out Carlee's life.

She didn't want anyone to know she was here for reasons he couldn't begin to understand yet, but he didn't want her interrupted while she explained herself. She was fragile. An interruption might shut her down completely.

He filled one cup with juice and the other with milk before handing her both.

She smiled as she took them from him, her eyes lighting up. There was a flush on her cheeks, and she glanced down at her lap. "I couldn't decide. I ate half of both."

He chuckled as he pulled the chair out from the desk and sat. He'd rather snuggle up to her on the bed, but for right now, he needed coffee, juice, and food. "That's fine, Baby girl. Do you want more? Eat them both if you'd like." She had carefully eaten exactly half of each. Adorably.

She patted her stomach. "No. I'm stuffed. I'm not used to eating so much." She tipped the milk cup back and sucked on the sippy lid. The sound warmed his heart further. He was glad she wasn't embarrassed to be Little in front of him.

He watched her drink as he ate one half of the sandwich in two bites, sipping his coffee in between. When the milk was gone, she picked up the juice and started on it.

Finally, she lowered that cup to her lap and stared at her crossed legs.

Atlas waited for her. She needed some time to collect her thoughts. He needed some time to stare at her and absorb everything he'd realized in the last hour.

She was his. Of that there was no doubt. Now, what to do about it. He struggled to wrap his mind around the revelation, but right now he needed answers. He didn't need to dump on her and add to her stress. She was obviously under enough stress without him adding to it.

When she lifted her face, it was streaked with tears.

Atlas jumped to his feet and came to her. He lifted her into his arms and carried her across the room to the armchair in the corner. He cradled her in his arms and leaned her head against his shoulder, stroking her cheek.

She cried hard, the sobs increasing.

"That's a good girl. Let it all out." He could do nothing but soothe her until she was able to speak. Her tears soaked the front of his shirt. He didn't care. He'd always hated seeing a Little in pain even when he'd been barely old enough to know he was a Daddy himself. But this pain his Baby girl was feeling tore him apart.

When her tears subsided, he rose, carried her into the bathroom, set her on the vanity, and wet a washcloth so he could wipe her face. He held a tissue up next. "Blow, Baby girl."

She glanced at him, blinking as if she couldn't believe he would care for her like this. That hurt him too. He realized someone had hurt her. How had it not occurred to him before now?

After several tissues, she was finally worn out from the exertion of crying. She'd needed it though. It was obvious she'd been holding it in for a long time. She'd been alone for a while too, and he fucking wanted to know why.

He carried her back to the armchair, settled himself, and adjusted her so she was straddling him. He wanted her close, and he wanted to be able to see her face.

With one hand spread against the small of her back, he used the other to tip her chin back. "Do you need your inhaler, Baby girl?"

She took a deep breath and then shook her head. "I rarely need it anymore. I mostly outgrew it as I got older."

"Okay. You'll let me know if you need it. Now, talk to me, Baby girl. Tell me everything."

Her bottom lip trembled. "You'll be mad."

That surprised him. "I promise I will not be mad. How could I be mad? I just arrived yesterday. Whatever is bothering you extends back way longer than that."

She swallowed. "But the club…"

"What about the club?"

"You're a tight group. Including you. I bet they brought you right back into the fold and didn't blink an eye. You're a member for life. I'm nobody. Just a girl from the wrong side of the tracks who happened to meet your sister in kindergarten."

She was rambling, and he had no clue what she was talking about, but he needed patience with this Little one. He lifted one of her hands and threaded their fingers together before bringing their combined hands to his mouth and kissing her knuckles.

He held her hand against his chest next. "The club is tight, Baby girl. That's a given, but I'm going to need you to be brave and tell me what has you so flustered. I can't fix it until I know what it is."

She bit her lower lip again, tearing at his heart. Finally, she released it and met his gaze "I was dating Silver for a while."

He tried not to react. His chest tightened at the thought of Carlee dating anyone at all, but it wasn't rational. She was twenty-five. Atlas hadn't been here. Of course she'd dated other men.

The truth was Atlas didn't know Silver well. The man was a few years older than Atlas, and Atlas had mostly left the fold when he was eighteen. What he did know was that Silver had disappeared a few weeks ago, and he'd been the treasurer.

Atlas suddenly stopped breathing. Was she crying because Silver had left? Was she in love with him?

Atlas needed to rein in his disappointment and control his reaction. If Carlee was in love with another man and Atlas had been reading her wrong for the past eight hours, there was nothing he could do about it. But he certainly wasn't the right person to console her.

"You miss him..." Atlas let his voice trail off as realization dawned.

Carlee flinched, her eyes going wide before she shook her

head. "No. I don't. He's…" She looked away. "I'm glad he's gone."

Atlas took a few seconds to absorb her words and let his heart restart before he licked his lips. "Did you break up?"

"Several months ago."

"I'm confused, Baby girl. You're going to have to give me more information."

She pulled her hand free of his and twisted her fingers together in front of her. "I shouldn't be telling you this," she murmured.

He frowned. *Telling me what?* "Carlee, look at me."

She shook her head defiantly like the Little girl she was.

"Carlee Marie, look at Daddy."

She gasped as she jerked her gaze to his. Her mouth fell open.

Now he had her attention. "Good girl. Now, let's get a few things straight." He hesitated, making sure she was listening. "First of all, you're *my* Little girl. I know it deep in my soul. Do you understand me?"

She slowly shook her head. Not so much in denial as in shock.

He smiled. "You are. Mine, Baby girl. I don't know how I managed to visit here even for a single day in the past few years and not notice this fact, but I'm here now, and it's as plain as day. You're mine."

She blinked. She was trembling. She didn't believe him. That was okay. He would prove himself to her.

"So, here's the thing. Whatever problems you've had in the past or are still having, they're my problems now. I will fix them. I will make you happy if it's the last thing I do. I can't stand to see your heart all tight and scared and hurting."

New tears fell down her cheeks, but he reached up to wipe them away.

"You can't be my Daddy. You don't live here."

He chuckled. "We'll figure that part out together, but right now we need to talk about what's so heavy on your soul. What happened with Silver?"

Her lip trembled again. "You won't believe me." Her tiny voice shook.

"I *will* believe you, Baby girl. I promise. I expect you to always tell me the truth, and that starts now."

She slowly drew in a breath. "He…" She shuddered. "He was always so liked in the club. He was so fun and made people laugh. When he started flirting with me, I thought maybe I'd finally found a Daddy within the club. That's all I ever wanted."

Atlas kept his temper in check. Something was going to go very awry with this story, and his Little girl needed him to keep his cool. He also had to deal with the jealousy that flared up. Someone else had claimed his Baby girl because he hadn't been here to do so himself. "Go on."

"He took me out on dates. Movies and dinners and dancing. I thought he really liked me. So, I moved in with him. About six months ago. He insisted. He had a house about a mile from here. Or has, I guess. I had a job at the library, but he wanted me to quit. He changed after I moved in with him. He was very possessive and didn't like me to leave the house. He didn't even let me go to the store. He sold my car. He said I didn't need other friends. I had him. He didn't even let me see Remi."

Atlas breathed deep and slow. He fisted one hand on his knee behind her where she couldn't see. "Go on, Baby girl. Tell me everything."

"He started shouting at me. I couldn't do anything right. He was always mad about when I had dinner ready or how I cleaned the house. I had thought he was the Daddy of my dreams. He tricked me, and then I was stuck. I had nothing. Less than nothing. I think he took advantage of that fact and thought he could control me because I didn't have a choice."

Atlas could barely keep himself in check. He wanted to

scream, but that wouldn't help Carlee out at all. He tamped down his frustration, his fists tightening behind her. "Did he hit you, Little one?"

She swallowed and looked away, new tears forming.

Atlas gritted his teeth. "Tell me specifically, Little one," he encouraged as calmly as he could manage.

She shook her head. "Don't wanna."

God, he loved the way her voice went so very Little. He hated the reason, but he liked the tone and the fact that she trusted him enough to be that Little with him. Even if it wasn't conscious.

She turned back toward him. "I shouldn't have told you any of this. The Shadowridge Guardians are tight. They stand up for their own. They'll never believe me, and why should they? Why would anyone believe me? I'm just a stupid girl from the wrong side of the tracks. A nobody." Her voice rose. "I can't even keep myself afloat. I was behind on my rent. I'm not qualified to do anything but clean toilets or waitress. Even my car is broken down."

Atlas slid his hands to her back and held her firmly. "Listen to me, Carlee Marie. I'm going to say this one time and one time only. You are not nobody. You are a bright, funny woman with a beautiful, kind spirit. I've known that most of my life. You might have been born into circumstances beyond your control, but that's not your fault. You will not talk down about yourself. If I hear you doing so again, I will spank your bottom so hard you won't be able to sit for a week. And don't think I've forgotten that I already owe you a good hard spanking." He lifted a brow.

Her cheeks turned pink, she bit her bottom lip, and she squirmed on his lap. Was she aroused?

"I promise I will help you get your finances straightened out. Whatever money you owe or any bills you need paid are now my responsibility, and I will handle them. Later today, you can go over your finances with me, and I'll take care of the rest."

She gasped. "You can't do that."

"I can, and I will. It's what Daddies do."

"You're not my Daddy." She pouted.

He narrowed his gaze at her. "I believe I already established the fact that I am indeed your Daddy, Baby girl."

"Surely you didn't mean that," she whispered.

"I meant every word. You. Are. Mine." He gave her a little shake. "And lastly, I absolutely do believe you about what happened with Silver, and everyone else in the club will believe you too or they can answer to me."

She took short shallow breaths. "You do?" Her voice wobbled, and she swiped at renewed tears.

"Every word. I'm sure you're not the only Little girl he took advantage of. Abusers always have a string of women they've conned. I'll get to the bottom of it. But it's important for you to understand that it's not your fault."

She shook her head. "It's totally my fault. I should have known. I should have left sooner. I should have…"

He squeezed her ass with his palms. "Stop that. You were vulnerable, and Silver took advantage of it. Besides, apparently you did leave, didn't you?"

She nodded slowly.

"Tell me how that happened."

"When he hit me."

"How many times did he hit you, Baby girl?" Atlas hated to hear the answer, but he needed to, and he needed to look her in the eye while she responded. He needed to be her rock.

"Only once. He came home drunk. He was really late, and he got mad that dinner was cold. He'd told me to have it ready by six, and then he arrived at eleven in a rage. I had the food warming in the oven for a long time, but it was getting burned, and I didn't know which would be worse, so I turned it off, and when he got there, he went crazy, screaming at me. He threw the pan of food across the room. The glass dish shattered and the burned food went flying all over the kitchen." She drew in a deep breath and continued. "And then he backhanded me so hard. I didn't see it coming. My body went flying. My head slammed into the drywall so hard it left a mark, and I nearly passed out as I slid to the floor."

Atlas was certain his nostrils flared. "I'm so sorry, Baby girl. What happened next?"

"He stomped out of the house. I gathered what few things I had, stuffed them in a grocery bag, stole some of his cash from where he kept it in the tank of the toilet, and took off."

My God.

"I'm so proud of you. That was very brave. Why didn't you come to the club or to Remi?" He knew she hadn't even told Remi because no way would Remi have kept something like that from him or their father.

Her lip trembled. "No one would have believed me, and I didn't want to risk him coming after me if I talked bad about him. I was scared enough as it was that he would hunt me down. I assume he let everyone believe I was still living with him."

That made sense. Atlas was beginning to understand her perspective. He hated it, but she had good logical reasoning. "Where did you go?"

"I went to the motel on the edge of town for the first few nights. I paid in cash and never left my room. I was hurt. I knew I had a concussion. I needed to sleep and wait for my head to stop hurting. I was nauseous and couldn't hold anything down."

He frowned. "You needed a doctor," he pointed out unnecessarily. He realized she could have died.

"I didn't have insurance or money, Atlas. I didn't have anyone. It was just me. Alone. All I had was my determination not to let him win."

"You're such a brave, strong girl, Carlee. I'm so proud of

you." He rubbed her back. There was nothing he could say to make up for the trauma she'd endured all alone, but starting now he would make sure nothing like that ever happened to her again. She would never be alone. She would have him, Remi, his father, and the entire fucking MC at her back. "I want Doc to look at you to make sure you're okay."

She sighed. "It was months ago. I'm fine. I don't need a doctor now."

He disagreed, but he needed to listen to the rest of the story. "We'll discuss it again later. Tell me the rest. You only stayed at the motel two nights?"

"Yes. On the third day I finally felt well enough to go outside. I was scared to even open the door for fear Silver would be waiting for me and kill me. But he wasn't. He could have easily found me there if he'd tried. It's not like there are very many places I could have gone. All he would have needed to do was ask at the front desk. But he didn't, and that made me think maybe, just maybe he wasn't going to bother me."

That didn't seem likely. There had to be more. If Silver was a serial abuser, which Atlas assumed was the case, he wouldn't let her walk away.

Carlee sniffled. "There's more."

He figured. "Go on."

"I needed a job, and it just so happened that Marv had an opening at the diner. I took it. I went to the junk yard where Silver had sold my car next. They felt sorry for me and let me buy it back. I knew it was a piece of shit, but it at least ran. I slept in it for two weeks until I got paid, and then I used the money from my check to get the studio apartment."

"I do not know anyone as strong and determined as you, Baby girl," he praised. He was seriously in awe of how much she'd done to get her feet back under her.

"I wasn't ever able to pay the rent after that. My car kept needing repairs, and I needed to eat and keep the water bill and electricity paid. So, I was behind from the moment I moved in. I knew I was in a heap of trouble when my car stopped running last night."

"So you've been barely holding your head above water for three months? Why didn't you call Remi, Little one?" He didn't understand that part. The two of them had always been tight.

She sighed. "Because it turned out Silver didn't just let me go. He was waiting for me outside my apartment one night about a month after I left him. Scared me to death. I turned around and tried to run, but he caught me. Slammed me against the wall, got in my face, and threatened me. He said the only reason he was going to let me go was because I was a worthless piece of shit not worth his time, but if I ever told a single person, including Remi, he would make my life a living hell."

Carlee sucked back a gut-wrenching sob, and continued, "Remi sent me texts. I knew I couldn't put her off forever, so I finally texted her back and told her I was busy with a new job. Eventually, she would have hunted me down, but I've managed to put her off until now."

Atlas wanted to kill Silver. If he got his hands on him, he just might. But the man wasn't worth it. It would be much better to gather information, nail him to the wall for everything he'd ever done, and let him rot in prison for the rest of his life. There was no doubt the man had a trail of crimes behind him, his mysterious disappearance from the MC among them.

As soon as Atlas got Carlee calmed down and straightened out enough that she was no longer in a panic and scared for her life, Atlas would dig deep into the MC's finances and get answers. He was now certain the treasurer hadn't simply taken off and not returned. The fucker had undoubtedly committed several crimes.

His Little girl started shaking, and her face was pale. She licked her dry lips. "I said too much," she murmured.

He cupped her face with both hands and held it so she was looking him in the eye. "You did not say too much. I can't reiterate enough how much you mean to me and how proud I am for you trusting me. You can trust me and the entire club. I promise you."

Her eyes went wide. "You can't tell everyone, Atlas. He'll kill me."

Atlas was smart enough to know that initially she was correct. He needed to be selective until he had more information. "I won't tell the entire club yet, Baby girl, but I need to talk to my dad and Steele and Kade. They need to know. Trust me?"

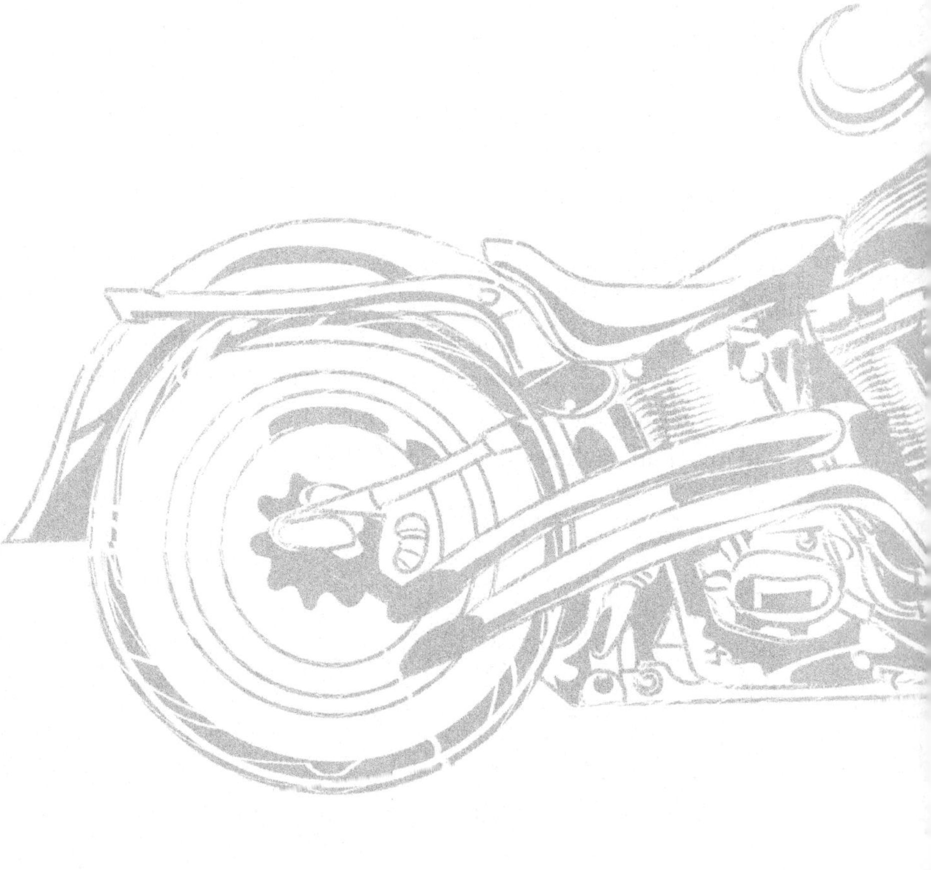

CHAPTER
SIX

Carlee couldn't breathe. She trusted Atlas, but he didn't understand. Silver was a mean, vindictive asshole. If he found out she was here at the club let alone told anyone what had happened...

Atlas held her face. "Deep breaths, Baby girl. Eyes on mine."

She tried to pull in a breath, but it got caught. She shouldn't have said all of that. It was reckless. But also what choice did she have? And Atlas said she was his. She should trust him. She did. Didn't she?

"Nothing is going to happen to you, Carlee. I promise. Daddy is going to handle it. You're not alone." He set his forehead against hers. "Breathe with me."

When he slowly inhaled, she did so too. As he exhaled, she did it with him. Several times.

"Good girl. Do you know what I want to do now?"

She shook her head subtly against his.

"Kiss you. May I?"

She gave him a slow smile. "Yes, please."

She barely finished speaking before his lips were on hers.

He wasted no time deepening the kiss as if he were

starving and she was his lifeforce. They went from zero to a hundred in seconds, him angling her head to the side, his tongue sweeping in to tangle with hers.

His hands were firm on her head, holding her where he wanted her. Claiming her. Making her forget her problems. Making her feel special and loved and important and Little.

When he finally released her lips, he didn't release her face. His huge hands were still holding her in place against him. They were both panting. He was smiling. "Do you believe me?"

She bit her bottom lip. What did he want her to believe? Which part? Her brain was scrambled.

"Whose Little girl are you, Carlee?"

Her breath hitched. She stared at him. "Yours, Daddy." God, that felt good. It sounded good too.

His smile told her how pleased he was. "That's right. Will Daddy let anything happen to you?"

"No," she whispered.

"Who's going to protect you?"

"You are, Daddy." She wanted to believe him so badly. She was saying the words, but she knew her doubts would creep back in soon.

"Here's what's going to happen next, Baby girl. I'm going to strip your jeans off, take you over my knees, and spank your bare bottom. I'm going to do so for two reasons. One is because you owe me a long hard spanking for all the swats you've accumulated in the past eight hours. But also because it will help you release the pent-up stress you're carrying around. Do you understand?"

She gave a slight nod. She was nervous, but her heart was also racing at the same time. She wanted him to spank her. She'd dreamed of being spanked by Atlas for years. Long before she'd been old enough to say a word or understand her true feelings.

She'd been a freshman in high school when she'd first

started fantasizing about Atlas taking her over his knees and spanking her bare bottom. Did he know this was a dream come true?

"Yes, Sir," she told him in the strongest voice she could muster.

"Has anyone ever spanked you before, Baby girl?"

She shook her head.

His brows lifted. "No one?"

"No, Sir." She'd been hanging around this club filled with Daddies and Littles for most of her life. It was in her blood. But she hadn't had her own Daddy until stupid Silver started wooing her. But Silver hadn't been a Daddy at all. He'd been an abuser. He hadn't ever treated her the way she'd watched other Daddies at the club treat their Littles.

Silver didn't have the Daddy gene at all. He'd faked it with his friends. He'd told everyone he was her Daddy and claimed her, but he had sequestered her in his house as more like an indentured servant.

He'd fucked her too. Often. But he'd never taken the time to take care of her. He'd simply taken from her and left her wanting.

She shook that thought from her head. Silver didn't belong in this room. She was with Atlas now. She already knew he was a good Daddy. She already felt ten times more for him than she'd ever felt for Silver. A hundred times more. She rocked forward, feeling his cock against her pussy, wondering if he would have sex with her too. Did he even want that kind of relationship with her?

Her face heated at the thought. Maybe he didn't think of her in a sexual way. But that made no sense. Of course he did. He'd just kissed her so long and hard she would never forget it.

He chuckled and lifted her off his lap to stand her in front of him. "Naughty girl. You need a spanking right now. It will be on your bare bottom. Daddy is going to see every inch of you. But you won't come. Not this morning. You need to focus on your punishment. If you're a good girl and prove to me that you trust me, I'll rub your little pussy later." He lifted a brow.

She bit her lip hard. His words made her panties wet, and he was going to see that when he took them off. She was embarrassed. Maybe she could take them off herself, keep them in her jeans as she removed them so he wouldn't notice.

"Tell me you understand, Baby girl."

"I understand, Daddy."

He reached for the front of her jeans, but she took a step back to unbutton them herself. "I can do it."

He swatted her hands away. "Did I ask you to do it, Baby girl?"

Her face heated further. "No, Sir." Calling him Sir was suddenly flowing so naturally from her mouth. It felt innate.

"From now on, I will dress you and undress you. You will not pick your clothes, nor will you decide when to put them on or take them off. Understood?"

She couldn't move. He was serious. He was going to see her naked. What if he didn't like her body? "I can pick my own clothes," she murmured, feeling like she should at least push back a bit.

"I'm certain you can. I assume you've been doing so without issue for twenty-five years. I bet you've managed to go to work appropriately dressed without a single issue." He grinned, teasing her.

She nodded.

"But now you don't have to anymore." He grabbed her hips and pulled her closer between his legs. His voice was lower when he continued. "There are a lot of things you don't have to do anymore. Because now you have a Daddy who wants to do those things for you."

She leaned into him and set her forehead against his shoulder. She loved the way he rubbed her back and kissed the top of her head. But he needed to understand something, and she righted herself to courageously meet his gaze. "You're going to make me get used to you, and then you're going to leave me."

She barely held back her tears.

He shook his head. "No, Baby girl. Never. I'm never going to leave you."

"But you have a job in the city. You have a life and an apartment and friends and and and…"

He shook his head again. "I don't have all the answers yet, Baby girl, but I know one thing for certain. You're mine, and where I go, you go."

"I can't go to the city, Atlas." Her voice rose. "I live here. I'm simple and I—"

He cut her off. "You are not simple. You are a bright, intelligent girl. I don't think I ever saw you without a book in your hands when you were young. That's why you were working at the library, isn't it? Because you love books and learning."

She sniffled. He was right, but that didn't make her equipped for the city.

"We have a lot of things to deal with in the next few days. I need to understand what Silver was up to. I need to make sure you're safe and protected. I need to firmly establish myself as your Daddy so you won't doubt me. We will address the future soon, but it's not on the top of the list right now. Okay?"

How could she argue with that? "Okay."

He slid his thumbs up to her ribcage and gave her a tickle. "Okay what?"

She couldn't stop the giggle that escaped her lips as she tried unsuccessfully to wiggle free of him. "Okay, Daddy," she exclaimed.

"Who's in charge?"

She sighed. "You are, Daddy."

"Good girl." His hands came to the hem of her T-shirt. "Arms up."

She gasped. "Why are you taking my shirt off?"

He leaned in to kiss her briefly. "Because I've decided

you'll take your spanking naked, Baby girl. Would you like to argue about it and spend some time standing in the corner with your red-hot bottom on display after I'm done? Or would you like to cooperate with Daddy?"

She shuddered as she lifted her arms. He was so firm and intense while also being soft at the same time. He didn't raise his voice or indicate he was in any way angry, but he also didn't back down. She was pretty sure he meant what he said. If she kept arguing with him, she would end up naked in the corner.

He pulled her shirt over her head and then unfastened her bra.

She couldn't bring herself to meet his gaze. What if he didn't like what he saw?

"Carlee…"

She swallowed, keeping her face to one side.

"Look at Daddy."

Damn him. Was he psychic?

She turned her head slowly back toward him.

His thumbs stroked the sides of her breasts. "You are the most beautiful, sexy woman I've ever seen. I'm so fucking pleased to have had enough sense knocked into me to realize you're mine. Your body is perfection. My cock is hard just thinking about worshipping these precious nipples later today."

She was breathing heavily by the time he finished his speech. He really did know exactly the right things to say. And she couldn't wait for him to touch her nipples, but apparently that wasn't going to happen right now.

His hands came to the front of her jeans so he could pop the button and lower the zipper. He tugged the denim and her panties down at the same time, bending lower as he removed them.

"Hold on to my shoulders, Baby girl."

She grabbed his shoulders to balance herself while he

pulled first one leg off and then the other before also removing her socks. After tossing her clothes aside, he slid his hands up her body until they rested on her hips.

She held her breath. Was she pretty enough? Was he pleased? He'd said so already, but it was hard to believe him. It would be hard to believe anyone after three months with Silver.

She hated that he'd warped her self-esteem in such a short time, but he had managed to do a lot of damage quickly by constantly berating her. Her hips were too narrow. Her tits were too small. Her cunt wasn't wet enough. Her legs weren't long enough. Her hair was too messy. Her lips were too thin.

The list was long.

"Carlee…" Atlas's voice jerked her back to the present.

She met his gaze.

"Where did you go, Baby girl?"

She shrugged, feeling her face heat.

"Who are you with?"

"You, Daddy."

"Repeat after me." He squeezed her hips. "I'm beautiful."

"Daddy…" she moaned. This was silly.

"Do it, Carlee. Repeat after me. Now. I'm beautiful."

She sighed. He was relentless. "I'm beautiful," she murmured.

"My body is perfect."

She rolled her eyes. "My body is perfect," she muttered.

"Hey now. You aren't saying that with conviction."

She pursed her lips.

He kissed her nose. "We'll work on it. I bet that asshole told you things that aren't true, didn't he?"

She slowly nodded.

"In your heart, you know he was wrong."

She tried to nod again. Did she know that? Yes. She did. If she thought back to before she'd been with Silver, she knew she'd had more self-esteem.

"How about we get this spanking over with, yeah?"

She gave him a slight grin. "You want me to agree to a spanking?"

He chuckled in return. "Baby girl, after I spank your naughty bottom, you're going to feel so relieved that you'll probably conjure up all kinds of ways to misbehave this afternoon in an effort to get that same kind of high again."

She frowned. What was he talking about? "That's silly."

"You'll see." He guided her to one side and lowered her over his lap.

Her small breasts were flattened by his thigh. Her legs weren't long enough to reach the floor.

"Reach your hands to the small of your back. I'm going to hold your wrists there so they won't get in the way. I don't want to accidentally swat them and injure you."

She felt decidedly more vulnerable as she gave him her hands. He was fully dressed, and she was naked. It was unnerving while at the same time her pussy was wet and ached in a way she'd never experienced.

"I will start slow and let you get used to the feeling of being spanked, but I'm not going to go easy on you. A good hard spanking helps Little girls purge their icky feelings."

She couldn't wrap her head around that. She'd read about Littles getting their bottoms spanked, but she had no frame of reference to fully understand. Sort of like someone explaining what sex felt like. There had been no way to understand what it would be like to have her pussy filled tight with a man's cock until it had happened, and even then, she'd still failed to understand the appeal.

It kind of worried her. She'd had sex with a few boys in high school and soon after, but it hadn't made the earth shake. And Silver certainly hadn't caused her heart to beat faster or her blood to pump harder.

The first man to ever elicit even some of those sensations was Atlas, and truth be told, the most aroused she'd ever felt was right now across his lap with his hand rubbing her bottom, the anticipation of something entirely different from sex causing her nerves to go into overdrive.

Finally, he lifted his palm and swatted her bottom. She flinched but it didn't hurt. Not too bad. She could tolerate it.

He swatted her again, and again, and again. Several times in a row, just hard enough to make her take notice. Not hard enough to do more than sting.

"Such a good girl," he praised as he paused to rub her bottom again. The intimacy almost made her swoon. "I'm going to spank you harder now, Little one. Try to relax your body. It will hurt more if you clench your butt cheeks."

She whimpered as he started again. It was impossible to obey him. She knew her butt was tight. Her entire body was stiff.

The sting increased. It started to burn. He spanked her with no rhyme or reason, switching cheeks and thighs at random. He covered every inch of her skin from the top of her bottom to almost the backs of her knees.

When he paused to rub her heated skin again, she was panting. She squeezed her legs together. Arousal made her pussy tingle. It was embarrassing. Why was she aroused? It made no sense.

"Part your thighs, Baby girl."

She couldn't. She would die if he found out she was aroused.

"Carlee..." he warned. "Spread your legs for Daddy. I know you're wet. Does that embarrass you?"

She whimpered and nodded.

"I don't want you to ever be embarrassed by your body's reaction to me, Carlee. Little girls often get aroused when their Daddies spank them. It's normal. It's intimate, and as you let your worries go it's common for you to feel closer to me and want contact with your pussy."

Was that true? He wouldn't tell her so if it weren't true.

He patted her thighs. "Legs, Carlee. Last warning. If I have to part them myself, I'll swat your pussy, and I don't think you're ready for that yet."

She gasped as she spread her knees. It felt awkward and left her so exposed. But this was Atlas. Not a stranger. He cared about her. He was treating her with more kindness than she'd ever received in her life even while he spanked her. He did so with respect and love. He did so presumably to help her feel better.

It might have been working. She wasn't sure yet, but she did know she wanted him to continue.

"Are you ready for more, Baby girl?"

"Yes, Daddy," she admitted softly.

He resumed, swatting her harder and faster.

It was difficult to catch her breath or think about anything except the burn building in her bottom. Her legs trembled. Her pussy was dripping. She had the urge to rub her nipples against his thigh, but she didn't dare.

Suddenly, something snapped inside her and she started crying, deep uncontrollable sobs that wouldn't stop. Tears ran down her face and dripped onto the floor. Her nose was running. She was full on ugly crying within minutes.

The last few swats were hard enough to make her cry out, and then he was done. He immediately rolled her over and cradled her against his chest. He rubbed her back and kissed her temple, whispering words she couldn't hear.

She kept crying and crying. Her tears and snot were saturating his shirt for the second time this morning. She couldn't stop. He didn't try to get her to stop either. He just rubbed her back and rocked her.

When she was finally able to take some breaths between sobs, she heard some of his words. "Such a good girl." "My beautiful Little girl." "Let it all out, Baby." "You're so brave." He kept repeating all these nice things over and over.

Eventually her crying slowed down to the occasional hitch of breath and hiccup.

Atlas lifted the edge of his shirt to wipe her face. He smiled at her. "Feel better, Baby girl?"

She did. She nodded. "Tired," she admitted.

"That's normal. Like I said, a good spanking helps Little girls purge their icky feelings. You'll probably feel drained and need a nap afterward."

She hiccupped again. "Will it always be like that?"

"Not always. Sometimes I'll just spank you hard and fast to discipline you and remind you who's in charge."

"I don't need discipline, Daddy. I'm a grown woman."

He smiled broadly, his body shaking with silent laughter. "Sweet girl, I've only been with you a few hours, and already I know you're going to need a lot of correctional spankings."

"I am not," she argued, pouting. "Why would I want you to spank my bottom?" She squirmed on his lap, every movement bringing attention to her heated skin. "It hurts."

"Because it also feels good. Because you feel more alive right now than you've ever felt. Because your pussy is throbbing with need." He lifted a challenging brow.

How did he know all of that? How embarrassing.

He chuckled again. "You're not the only Little girl alive who likes the way it feels to get spanked. The tingly burn. Every time you move for the rest of the day, you'll remember my palm on your sweet bottom and squirm, wondering when I'm going to do it again."

She frowned and shook her head. "No, I'm not," she lied.

He hugged her closer and kissed her nose. "My God, you are precious. Every delightful inch of you." He rose to his feet, holding her in his arms as if she weighed nothing.

She wasn't sure what his intention was, but he carried her to the bed and lowered her gently onto her side. After tucking Hammie and the new bear into her arms, he pulled the covers over her and kissed her temple. "You need a nice long nap, Baby girl."

"I don't take naps," she argued defiantly, her eyes heavy.

He shook his head. "You do now. You'll do what Daddy says because I know what's best for you." He rubbed her shoulder. "I need to go talk to my dad and find Steele and Kade so I can figure out what was going on with Silver. You will stay in this bed and nap while I'm gone, understood?"

She shivered at the firm tone of his voice. "Yes, Sir." It was impossible to disobey him. He commanded compliance.

"I will lock the door from the outside so you can rest easy knowing no one will come in this room but me."

"Thank you, Daddy." He was right. She would rest easier if she didn't have to worry about anyone finding her here in his bed. She twisted her neck to look at him. "You won't tell everyone I'm here yet, right?"

"No, Baby girl. Just Steele, Kade, my dad, and probably Remi. She caught me in the laundry room in the middle of the night. I blew her off, but I'm sure she's going to hunt me down as soon as she has the chance and grill me about who I had in my room."

Carlee whimpered. "She's going to be mad at me. *I've* blown her off for months."

"She'll understand. You've been friends for twenty years. When she finds out what happened, she will forgive you."

"Do you really think so?" She liked that he gave her so much hope.

"I know so, Baby girl. Don't you worry about Remi. She's going to be your biggest supporter."

"I've been mean to her." Carlee's lip trembled. "I sent her vague texts and ignored her calls before my phone died.."

"She'll understand. Do you even know she has a Daddy now?"

Carlee's eyes widened. She felt guilty for not knowing anything about her oldest friend, especially that. "No. Who?"

"Kade. They're very happy."

"That's great." Carlee smiled as she pictured her friend with Kade. She couldn't wait to hear about it.

"One more thing, Little one. Look at Daddy. This is important."

She tipped her head back, wondering what else he needed to say. She was so tired.

"Your orgasms are mine, Baby girl. You will not touch your pussy without permission. Keep your naughty fingers away from your swollen clit and tight channel when I leave this room."

Her face heated a hundred degrees. How did he know her pussy was so wet and needy? How did he know she was literally shaking with the need to come? "Daddy..." she complained.

"I mean it. I'll know if you touch yourself. You won't be able to lie to me. Your pleasure is mine to dole out now. You will not masturbate unless I tell you it's okay and I'm watching."

She gasped. "You can't watch me masturbate," she exclaimed.

He lifted his brows.

"Daddy!"

He still said nothing.

She groaned and turned her face into the pillow. That only made things worse. It was the pillow he'd laid his head on last night. It smelled like him.

"What's my rule?"

She shook her head and muttered into the pillow, "I heard you."

"Look at me and tell me the rule."

Was he really going to make her say it? Did he realize she was squeezing her thighs together because the humiliation was making her arousal spike even higher?

Yes, he did. Damn him.

"I'm waiting."

She drew in a deep breath and met his gaze. He wasn't going to give up until she did. "I won't touch myself."

"I won't touch my pussy, Daddy," he corrected. "I won't play with my nipples either."

Flames set her face on fire. He was good. Devious and so very good at this Daddy thing. "I won't touch my pussy or play with my nipples, Daddy."

"Good girl." He leaned over and kissed her briefly on the lips. "Sleep, Baby girl."

She watched as he left the room and listened to the sound of the lock engaging as he did everything he could to make her feel safe. Her heart raced for several minutes as she stared at the door and tried to process the one-hundred-eighty-degree turn her life had taken. It was too much to absorb though, and she finally closed her eyes and let sleep drag her under.

CHAPTER SEVEN

"You wanted to see me?" Steele said as he entered the meeting room in the clubhouse.

Atlas was sitting at the big table, and he looked up at the final member of the club he'd been waiting on before he started talking.

Kade and his father were already present.

Rock nodded toward Steele. "I think you should shut the door."

Atlas was grateful. He'd only been back home for twenty hours. After a ten-year absence that brought him back only for short visits at holidays, there was no reason for the club president or the enforcer to grace him with their presence or be so quick to listen to what he had to say.

Atlas was grateful the members of this MC were not assholes who would ignore his request or lecture him on his audacity. He knew part of the reason they were showing him respect was because his father had been the one to call this meeting.

Even though Rock's health was questionable after a recent heart attack, he was held in high esteem among all the club members. That included Steele and Kade.

Steele looked concerned as he shut the door and took a seat. "Is everything okay?"

"No," Atlas admitted. No sense beating around the bush. He didn't want to be away from Carlee any longer than necessary. He didn't want her to wake up and panic and doubt everything she'd felt this morning. He knew her well enough after just a few hours of reacquainting himself with her that she would definitely wake up confused and uncertain. It was going to take time for her to truly trust him. It would take time for her to trust anyone after the way Silver had treated her.

Kade nodded. "Go on."

"I ran into Carlee Deveraux last night when I was out riding. Her car was broken down on the side of the road. I meant to give her a ride home, but one thing led to another, and I quickly realized she was in financial distress and all was not right in her world."

"We haven't seen Carlee around here in a while," Steele stated. "She started dating Silver about six months ago and stopped coming to the club. They broke up a few months ago, but Carlee didn't come back."

Atlas nodded. "So none of you have any idea what happened between Carlee and Silver, do you?"

"Only what he told us," Rock confirmed.

"Which was?" Atlas encouraged.

Kade leaned forward, planting his elbows on the table. "He did not come to Steele or me directly, but we heard murmurs among the members. Something to the effect that they had tried to make a go of it but then she'd decided she didn't want to be the girlfriend of an MC member. She'd wanted him to cut loose of the club and get a job outside of the compound."

Rock groaned. "I heard that too. It sounds absolutely ridiculous out loud."

Steele nodded and ran a hand down his face. "It does. I didn't think much of it. It was her choice. If she didn't want to come around anymore, we weren't going to get in her way."

Atlas leaned forward and looked each man in the eye. He didn't mean to be a dick but for fuck's sake. "No red flags? Carlee has been Remi's best friend and hanging around the club for twenty years. I suspect she's known she was Little for at least ten years. She was desperate to find a Daddy, and the moment she started dating a club member, no one thought to question her disappearance?"

"Son..." his father warned.

Steele shoved his chair back and stood. He turned to pace the room. "No, Rock. Atlas is right. We've been so caught up in trying to figure out what the hell was going on with the finances that none of us took the time to consider the implications of Carlee's disappearance."

"I know Remi tried to contact her," Rock stated. "Carlee blew her off. I should have questioned things further. I should have gone to talk to Carlee myself."

"We all should have," Kade agreed. "Where is she now?"

"My room."

No one flinched at that revelation.

"There are a few things I want to make perfectly clear," Atlas informed them. "Most importantly, Carlee is under my protection now. She told me everything that happened with Silver, and I believe her."

"Son?" Rock met Atlas's gaze dead on.

"She's mine."

Rock took a deep breath and nodded. "Does this mean—"

Atlas interrupted. "It means she's mine. Nothing more. One day at a time. I would prefer that her presence in my room remain a secret for the time being. It's going to take some time for her to trust anyone."

"Why doesn't she trust us?" Steele asked, leaning over the table and planting his hands on the surface. "She's practically family."

"She knows how tight club members are. She assumes Silver trash-talked her to anyone who would listen. She rightfully believes her name has been dragged through the mud among nearly everyone in the club. It doesn't matter that everything Silver said was probably a lie. She's scared and worried."

Kade nodded. "Understandable. Please extend our apologies to her. Our oversight was insensitive and unintentional. I will apologize myself when the chance arises, but in the meantime, would you tell her how sorry I am and reassure her she is a trusted member of this community?"

"Thank you. I will pass that on."

Steele and Rock nodded their agreement.

Atlas changed the subject to the next pressing issue. "I'm going to dig into every single thing Silver was managing and left behind. I bet I will find some troubling information that will reaffirm that the villain in this situation was not Carlee."

Steele nodded. "Whatever you need, you'll let us know. This matter is of the utmost urgency. Thank you for coming to straighten it out. I know this was an inconvenience for you and your life is elsewhere, but I'm sure I'm not going to be the only club member who secretly hopes you decide to stay."

"He's right," Kade agreed. "We won't stop you from doing what's best for you, but for Carlee's sake…"

Atlas leaned back in his chair. "One thing at a time, please. The situation with Silver is my current focus. No one has any clue where he is?"

They all shook their heads. "He hasn't been seen here or anywhere in town for two weeks. As far as we know, he also hasn't been to his house. He vanished. The only reason we haven't reported him as missing is because all of us suspect he was involved in something illegal. He was acting gradually more nervous and irritable for weeks."

"Did he hurt her, son?" Rock suddenly asked, changing the subject.

Atlas was waiting for that question. "Yes, but she's strong.

He only managed to hit her once. He made it count, but she never looked back when she left."

Rock sighed. "I'm so very sorry. Has she seen a doctor? You should have Doc look at her."

"No, she didn't have the money to pay for a doctor. I will speak to Doc soon. But most of the damage was inflicted to her self-esteem. Stereotypical abuser. Not a Daddy bone in his body," Atlas informed them.

"We should have known," Kade growled.

"Abusers hide their true selves well," Atlas pointed out. "This club is large. You can't know the behavior of every member in the privacy of their homes. Silver hid it well. He isolated her, made her feel worthless, separated her even from Remi, took her car, made her quit her job."

Steele drew in a deep breath. He didn't say anything else. It had all been stated already.

"When the time is right," Rock said, "we will make sure the entire club knows who was in the right here."

"Thank you. I appreciate your support. Carlee will too. She's been alone for months, worrying."

"I assume he threatened her?" Kade asked.

"Yes." Atlas stood. "I really need to go check on her and then dig into the mess I bet I'll find in Silver's office."

"You'll let us know if you need anything," Steele insisted.

"Yes. Thank you." Atlas moved to the door and opened it. He didn't even flinch when he found his sister standing in the hallway, leaning against the wall, arms crossed, eyes narrowed. She looked like she was ready to lay into him with twenty questions.

Remi hadn't changed a bit. She was just as Goth as she had been for years. Even her relationship with Kade hadn't changed her style. The fact pleased Atlas greatly. It meant Kade had no intentions of turning Remi into someone she was not.

She was currently wearing all black with dark eyeshadow

and heavy mascara. Though she did have that hot pink bow again. Atlas took a deep breath and met her gaze. "Remi."

Kade spoke from behind Atlas. "Princess, if you're waiting in that hallway to bother your brother, think again, Little girl. He's got things to do this morning. You can catch up with him later."

She shoved off the wall, rolling her eyes defiantly. Exactly the look Atlas had received from Carlee more than once in the last twelve hours. He almost smiled at their similarities. They were night and day in the style department, but the two of them had always been thick as thieves. They had similar looks and mannerisms like sisters.

"He's my brother," she declared, leaning over his shoulder to catch eyes with Kade. "I'm worried about him," she lied. When she turned back to Atlas, she whispered, "Who was the girl in your room last night? You weren't even home five minutes. How did you manage to bag a girl?"

"Remi Monroe," Kade thundered from behind Atlas before he materialized at his side and took his Little girl by the arm. "That naughty mouth of yours is going to land you in a heap of trouble. It's none of your business what Atlas does in his private time. You will not give him the third degree. Understood?"

She grumbled. "Fine. For now." She pointed at her brother. "But only because my butt hurts already. I'm going to find you later, and you're going to tell me what's going on with you."

Atlas nodded, fighting the urge to chuckle. His sister was eight years younger than him, just like Carlee. He'd always adored her, but she could be fierce when she wanted to be.

"Remi," Kade warned in a menacing voice. "You will not be nosy. No snooping around your brother's private life. If I find you near his room, I will spank you in the hallway and ask questions later. Do I make myself clear?"

"Yes, Daddy."

Atlas was fascinated watching his sister back down to her

Daddy. He hadn't been home since Remi and Kade had gotten together. He'd known she'd met her match, but seeing them in action was reassuring. Kade had her in hand, and Remi had him wrapped around her finger. They were the perfect pair.

"Come on. Let's go home," Kade said. "I think you need some time to think. You're not going to hang around the club all day snooping."

She groaned and dragged her feet as Kade guided her away from the meeting room.

Rock slapped Atlas on the back, chuckling. "Hard to believe, isn't it?"

"Very." Atlas watched the two of them as they disappeared around the corner. "But I'm so happy for her. We always knew she would be a handful. She's met her match."

"That's the truth." Rock turned toward Atlas. "I bet you're going to need all the help you can get. Go check on your girl first, and I'll meet you in Silver's office."

"Thank you. She's been burning the candle at both ends for a while. I suspect she'll sleep most of the day now that she's safe and protected. I'll look in on her and see you in a minute."

"Take your time."

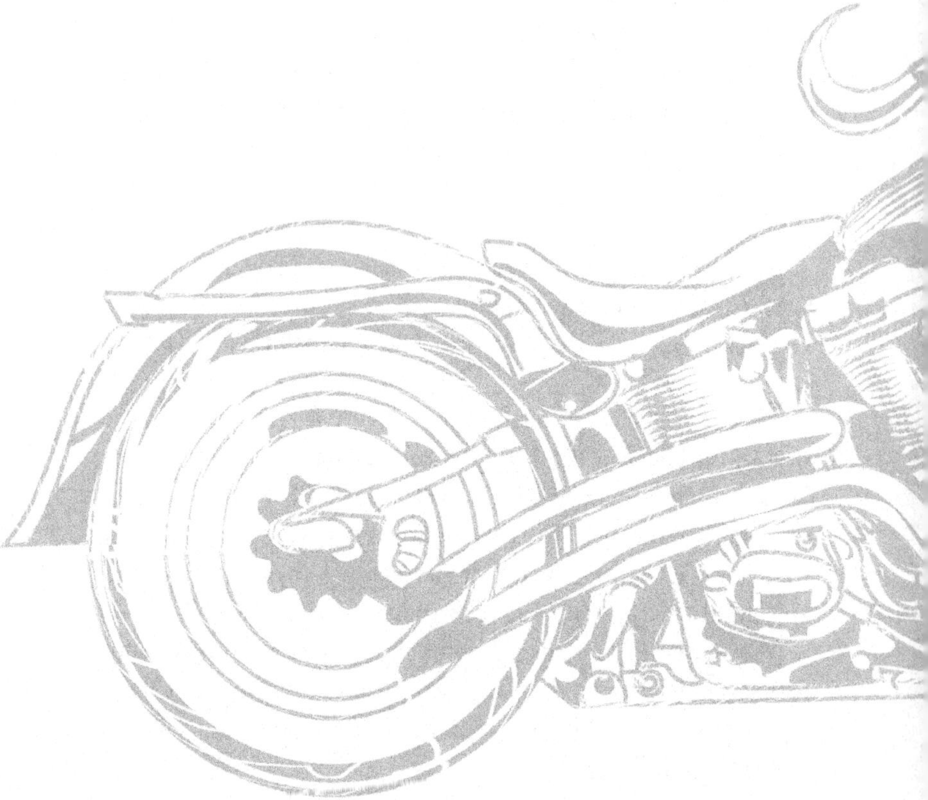

CHAPTER EIGHT

The sun was bright and leaking through the edges of the blinds when Carlee woke up. She glanced at the clock. It was late afternoon. She'd slept hard for most of the day. She still felt tired too. When she considered the fact that she wouldn't have even been off work yet, she shuddered.

After so many days of working long shifts and dealing with financial woes, car trouble, and mounting bills, she'd crashed hard.

It all seemed too good to be true.

The sheets felt amazing. They weren't super expensive or high thread count or anything, but they were nicer than any she'd had in months, and they were clean, and they smelled like Atlas, and she was naked.

She grinned. She was naked in Atlas's bed.

She vaguely remembered him checking on her a few times, but she'd been too groggy to do more than whimper and go back to sleep.

She smiled as the lock turned in the door a moment before it opened. It was so thoughtful of Atlas to keep it locked so she could rest knowing no one would discover her.

Atlas slipped inside. He was holding a brown paper bag,

and immediately the room filled with the scent of BBQ. "I thought you might be hungry."

She pushed to sitting, taking the covers with her so she wouldn't expose herself. "Starving." She hadn't realized it until that moment, but she was absolutely famished. She'd slept through lunchtime after eating breakfast really early in the morning.

Atlas set the bag on the desk before sitting on the edge of the bed. He cupped her face, stared into her eyes, and then kissed her. "Do you feel better after getting some sleep?"

She nodded. "Much better. Thank you." Now that she was awake, worries were creeping in though. Namely the fact that she didn't have a job, a car, or an apartment. "I need to get my car towed to the repair shop," she said as her brain ran down the list of responsibilities.

"I already took care of it. It's at the junkyard. It was only worth the value of the scrap metal, Little one."

Her eyes bugged out. "Atlas, I need that car. It's held on this long. It just needs some Band-Aids."

"Carlee, I had two guys look at it. It needed far more than a Band-Aid this time. There was a crack in the alternator. Several of the hoses are too worn to trust. The power steering is shot. Even if it could be repaired, I wouldn't let you drive it. It's not trustworthy or safe. You'd end up broken down on the side of the road again, and the next time it might not be me who finds you."

She clutched the covers at her chest, stiffening as she sat straighter. "I need to get a new job, and I'll need transportation. It gets me by." She had no idea what any of those things he listed were or how much the repairs would be.

Atlas drew in a slow breath. "Do you remember anything from this morning, Baby girl?"

She rolled her eyes. She remembered far too much from this morning. She squeezed her legs together at the mention.

Her bottom was still hot and tingly. Renewed wetness leaked from her pussy.

"Who's responsible for you now?" he asked.

She sighed.

He lifted her chin. "Look at me, Baby girl. Answer me."

"You are," she whispered, not fully believing that could be true.

"Do you think I'd ever let you drive in an unsafe vehicle?"

"Atlas…"

"Answer the question. What sort of Daddy would I be if I put you in that death trap?"

"It isn't a death trap. It's just quirky. It needs TLC."

"It needs a quick death. For now, you're not leaving the clubhouse without me. If you need to go somewhere, you'll do so on the back of my bike or in my car. Both of those will only be with me behind the wheel. I don't want you leaving here with anyone else for any reason, and certainly not alone. Understood?"

She frowned at him. Part of her thought she should climb out of his bed, demand that he give her some clothes, and stomp out of his room. He was so highhanded.

The problem was his stern demands made her feel both hot and bothered as well as cherished and loved.

"Are we clear?" he growled.

"Yes, Daddy," she responded sarcastically.

"Is that a nice tone to take with Daddy?"

She sighed heavily. "No, Sir." How had he gotten under her skin so deeply? She'd dreamed a thousand dreams of being dominated by this man for half her life, but none of her imaginations compared to the real deal. He was so much more… Daddyish. So commanding. He had a hold of her heart, and he had the power to break it.

He tugged at the covers. "Lie down on your tummy, Baby girl."

She gripped them tighter, not releasing them. Even though

he'd seen her naked this morning, she felt oddly shy and self-conscious about her body still. "Why?" Was he going to spank her again just because she was sassy with him?

"Because I want to check your bottom and make sure I spanked you with just the right amount of pressure."

She shook her head. "You don't need to do that. It's fine."

He narrowed his gaze. "Who will decide if your bottom is fine or not?"

She blew out a heavy breath. "Can you just take my word for it? I'm embarrassed."

He cupped her face. "I don't want you to be embarrassed with me, Baby girl. That needs to end right now. Your safety is my top priority, and that includes your skin's reaction to my palm. I'm going to be seeing your naked body often, so you need to get used to it. I will know every inch of you inside and out. I'll be the first to know even the subtlest of changes in your health and wellbeing." He lowered his hand, yanked the covers out of her grip, and pulled them out of the way. "Now, lie down before I start counting to three."

She scrambled to turn over and do as he said. It wasn't worth arguing about, and he would win anyway. Her breasts felt heavy pressed against the mattress, and her nipples were hard points that grazed the sheet beneath them, making her breath hitch.

Atlas set a hand on the small of her back as if restraining her. His other hand smoothed over her bottom as he leaned closer to inspect his work. "I like how this looks. The pink is just right for several hours after a spanking. I want you to still feel the burn, but I don't want your skin to bruise. When I spank you to correct your behavior, you should feel the reminder all day but not suffer any injury that lasts into the next day."

She turned her face away from him. She didn't say what she was thinking. That he probably wanted her to heal enough each day so he could do it again. And that idea made her cheeks heat.

He tapped the backs of her thighs. "Spread your legs, Baby girl."

She whimpered and shook her head against the pillow. *Not that. Please not that.*

"Carlee Marie. Part those thighs for Daddy right now."

She held her breath. More heat flooded her face. Luckily he couldn't see it, but in a moment he was going to find out how wet she was, and the idea mortified her.

"Wider," he ordered when she only parted her knees an inch.

She did as he commanded, but not without trembling with embarrassment.

"Good girl. You won't hide your body from me, Baby girl. Ever. Your physical reactions to my words and actions are an important part of our relationship." He slid a hand between her thighs, found her folds, and stroked through the copious wetness.

Carlee moaned. When she tried to arch her hips off the bed, he held her down with his other hand just above her butt crack.

"So wet for me..."

She pressed her face deeper, squeezing her eyes shut.

"You're going to be a handful, aren't you, Baby girl? So naughty and sassy with Daddy. Do you know why?"

She didn't dare move. All her focus was on his fingers toying with her entrance anyway. A moment later, she cried out when he found her clit and stroked it gently.

"This is why," he stated. "Naughty, sassy Little girls who misbehave do so intentionally because it makes their little pussies wet and needy."

She shook her head again in defiance. That made no sense. Why would she want to suffer this humiliation?

He chuckled. "You're so precious and so innocent for someone who grew up hanging around the MC. It's obvious you've never had a true Daddy who took care of your needs. I'm kind of glad. I don't have to be jealous of any other man who belongs to the Shadowridge Guardians. Your naivete is all mine. I get to watch you blossom and learn what it means to have a Daddy."

She curled her toes into the mattress and bore down, trying to get more contact with his fingers. It was hard to focus on his words with his fingers casually playing with her pussy.

She'd never been this horny, this wet, this needy. Not with anyone ever. Certainly not with Silver who'd been her only real boyfriend and the only man she could hold up as a standard for all future boyfriends.

Intellectually she'd known he was a bad man and a bad Daddy. But she'd had no point of reference until now. Until Atlas. Until this Daddy who insisted he was hers took control.

"I'm going to let you bury your face this one time because I know you're surprised and embarrassed and have so many thoughts running through your head, but in the future, you will look at Daddy and show me those pretty brown eyes when you come."

She bit her lip. She was definitely going to come if he kept that up, and the idea made her nervous. No one had ever made her come before. No one except her. She'd only done so alone. It had been a while because she needed a vibrator.

Atlas nudged her legs wider and slowly eased a finger into her channel. "So tight, Baby girl. Can you come like this with just my fingers?"

Her breath hitched. She really didn't want to answer him.

"Tell me, Little one. I want to know everything about you. Every tiny detail. Can you come from Daddy touching you?"

She swallowed and turned her head slightly away from him so she could mumble a response. "I... I don't know. Maybe. Yes?"

He leaned over and kissed her temple. "Okay. Let's see." He added a second finger and pressed his thumb against her clit. "So wet. So tight. Don't hold back, Baby girl. I want to hear you when you come. These rooms are well insulated. No one will know but me."

She'd always heard the men in the MC saying that, but until now she hadn't fully realized why they cared so much. Apparently Daddy types didn't like everyone in the compound to hear their Little girls scream.

Not that Carlee would scream. She never made any noises when she had sex. Granted, she'd never enjoyed anything about sex before, and she certainly hadn't uttered a sound any time she'd masturbated for fear she would get caught. Every place she'd lived had had thin walls.

Atlas pushed his fingers deeper. He twisted his hand until his palm flattened on her clit, grinding down, making her breath hitch.

She lifted her face off the pillow, fisted the sides, and breathed heavily. Holy shit. She was going to come. It was going to shatter her to pieces and ruin her for other men. She knew it. She could feel it deep inside her. A tight need gripped her hard and wouldn't let go.

It was scary. She felt out of control. Her legs stiffened. So did her arms. Her heart raced. Her mouth fell open. She could hear herself moaning, but she couldn't stop it.

Atlas thrust his fingers in and out of her, rubbing her clit hard at the same time.

She wanted to tell him to stop because she was so out of control. She felt helpless. A foreign force was ruling her body. It freaked her out.

And then she was there, right at the peak. Teetering. She knew it. It was going to be massive. And Atlas was going to witness it.

"Now, Baby girl. Come on Daddy's fingers."

That was all it took. She came so hard and so violently that her entire body quaked, jerking and writhing. Her scream filled the room. Her nipples felt sensitive as they dragged against the sheet beneath her with every movement because she was up on her elbows, head tipped back.

Atlas continued to stroke her inside and out as the tremors subsided. It seemed to last for minutes, though that wasn't reasonable.

Finally, she dropped her forehead to the pillow, panting and crazed. Stunned. And ruined.

Atlas eased his fingers out. She heard him sucking them clean before he gathered her in his arms, rolled her over, and cradled her against his chest. He rained kisses all over her face before resting his forehead against hers.

He stroked her back. "That was the best gift I've ever received in my life. You've never come with a man before, have you?"

She shook her head slightly. She was without words or coherent thoughts. All she knew was his touch, the way he held her as if she were precious. The feel of his rough beard against her as he nuzzled her, the scent of his shampoo or soap or something, the soft way his lips kissed her everywhere he could reach, his heavy breathing, and his erection pressing against her hip, straining against his jeans.

"You're mine, Baby girl," he murmured. "Every inch of you. Don't fight it. Know it in your heart. Let me be your man, your Daddy, your lover."

She snuggled into him, shaking and scared out of her mind.

He kissed the top of her head. "It's okay. You'll know. I can be patient."

After rocking her for several minutes, he leaned her back. "You need to eat, Baby girl."

"Can I have clothes?" she asked in a very Little voice. She glanced at the dresser where he'd piled up her clean clothes in the night. They were gone now. She frowned. "Where did they go?"

"I put them in the drawers. I unpacked my suitcase into the drawers too." He lowered her gently to the bed and rose to stride across the room where several unopened packages now resided near the door.

She pulled the covers up over her chest as she sat. "What's all that?"

"Things I ordered for you last night."

"Did you sleep at all?"

He chuckled. "Not much. I'm used to it. I can do amazing things during tax season. One night won't kill me."

He grabbed all the packages and brought them to the bed, depositing them haphazardly. "How about you wear one of my T-shirts while you eat, and then you can open the packages. I need to get back to work on the club's books soon."

Atlas strode back across the room, opened a drawer, and snagged a T-shirt. After returning, he shook it out. "Arms up."

She loved the way he dressed her. It made her feel cherished.

He sat on the desk chair. "How do you feel about Remi coming to entertain you for a while?"

She rubbed her temple. "I'm sure she's mad at me."

"I don't think Remi holds a grudge, Baby girl. And if you explain to her what happened, I bet you'll fix any hard feelings in less than a minute. You can't ignore your best friend forever."

She nodded. He was right. "Okay. You didn't tell her I'm here yet?"

He shook his head, grinning. "No, but she suspects I have a woman in this room. She's already badgered me twice to tell her who it is."

"What if she doesn't like me dating her brother?"

He chuckled. "We're not dating."

Her heart stopped. Her stomach sank at the same time.

He set a Styrofoam container on the desk and glanced at her. "Carlee?"

She swallowed. "Okay..." What the hell were they doing?

His eyes widened. "Oh, shit. You misunderstood." He

reached over and grabbed her hand. "We are so far past dating, Baby girl. Light-years. Call it whatever you want, but it's forever. Not for the weekend."

"Does that make me like your old lady?" she asked. It sounded silly.

He laughed again. "I guess, but that's the polar opposite of anything I'll ever call you."

She couldn't keep from smiling. Even if he was full of shit and living in a warped world. She could pretend for a while. It would keep her mind off her serious life problems. No car. No job. No home.

Atlas picked up a paper plate and filled it with several things from the Styrofoam container before handing it to her. "If there's anything you don't like, just leave it, Baby girl."

She took the fork he offered her next, her stomach grumbling as she lifted the first bite to her mouth. Pulled pork. It melted as soon as it hit her tongue. She moaned.

Atlas leaned forward and kissed her sticky lips. "I'll feed you BBQ every day if it makes you moan like that."

Her face heated. She shoveled another bite into her mouth, this time potato salad. "So good..."

"I'm glad you like it. I used to love this BBQ place when we were kids. My dad picked it up and brought it home for dinner sometimes."

"I ate it at your house when I was there," she murmured. She hadn't had it in a long time. It wasn't in her budget. Silver certainly never brought home takeout. And Lord knows when she was a kid, her mother never thought a single moment about feeding her only child.

He must have read her reminiscence. "When was the last time you spoke to your mom?"

She laughed. "The night before she left me on my eighteenth birthday. She didn't even get me a gift. She didn't even say goodbye. She just left a note in the trailer saying that she was off to live her life now that I was an adult.

She'd paid off the trailer. I guess that was my birthday present."

Atlas cringed visibly. "I'm so sorry. No one deserves that."

She shrugged. "I've always considered it more of a blessing. At least I didn't have to deal with her revolving door of boyfriends anymore. They were creepy, and I was always afraid one of them would make a move on me."

"You spent a lot of time here though, right? With Remi?"

"Yes. I'm not sure where I would be now if it weren't for Remi and your dad and the kindness of the MC. And my mom leaving lit a fire under me. I had just graduated from high school. I got several parttime jobs. I did okay for myself. I even managed to keep that rundown shitty trailer."

"Until Silver came along."

"Yeah. It was a piece of shit anyway, so it wasn't hard for me to fall for him and be convinced I didn't need it. I know it wasn't worth much, but I think he sold it and took the money." She lifted her gaze. "I think he owed people money, Atlas."

Atlas nodded. "I think you're right. From what I've been able to discern so far going through the mess of poorly organized paperwork, I'd say he was gambling. I'm pretty sure he also stole club money when he took off."

She swallowed her next bite. "I'm sorry. Do you think I could have done something different?"

He met her gaze and shook his head. "No, Baby girl. Not a chance. He manipulated and abused you. You're not at fault, nor could you have stopped it. You did exactly the right thing and got yourself out of there the first time he struck you. I'm sorry it came to that, but I'm so damn proud of you for getting out."

He'd said all that before, but she figured he might have to repeat it several times before she would believe him.

Atlas tossed his empty paper plate in the trashcan under the desk. He leaned forward, put his elbows on his knees, and set his hands on her legs. "I need to get back to going through everything. I don't like leaving you here alone, but I'm worried your safety is tied up in this mess. I want to get to the bottom of it."

"I'll be okay."

"Promise me you won't leave this room."

"I won't."

He lifted a hand and cupped her face. "Try that again."

"I won't, Daddy."

"Good girl. Now, I'm positive Remi is hanging around waiting to pounce on me the moment I step out of this room. Can I send her in?"

Carlee nodded. "Yeah."

He nodded toward the piles of packages scattered all over the bed. "You two can open this stuff together. If there's anything you don't like, set it aside and I'll return it."

"Okay."

He took her empty plate from her, tossed it in the trash, and surprised her by leaning over and flattening her to the bed. He kissed her shoulder and then her neck before trailing kisses to her lips. "Say that again, Carlee."

She giggled against his lips. "Say what, Daddy?"

He growled and kissed her fiercely, one hand coming to the hem of her T-shirt to slide under it and up her body. He covered her breast with his palm and flicked her nipple until she moaned.

When he released her lips, he hovered, still toying with her nipple. "You may try on everything in those packages and wear whatever you want, but don't put on a bra. I want your tits naked under your shirts and dresses. Save the bra and panty sets for when we go out in public."

"Yes, Sir." A chill raced down her spine at the idea of going without a bra. Her breasts were small and hardly noticeable, but she'd always worn a bra anyway. She'd feel naked without one.

She'd do it for him though. She also knew a lot of Littles

didn't wear bras. She supposed their Daddies didn't offer them one. They often wore youthful dresses that barely covered their panties too. She'd seen most every woman's panties in this club at one time or another, especially when they were in their Little space. Cute panties. Full cut with babyish designs and patterns. She glanced at the packages and wondered if Atlas had bought her panties.

She turned back to him. "I can't pay for all this, Atlas."

He narrowed his gaze. "I can't wait for you to realize you're mine." He kissed her lips again and then trailed kisses down her front, between her breasts over the T-shirt. It had ridden up a bit too high on her thighs when he'd shoved her to her back.

Atlas grabbed her wrists, held them at her sides, and kissed her inner thigh.

Carlee let out a shocked cry.

His mouth continued, nibbling a path up her inner thigh until he reached the apex of her pussy.

She flushed what had to be a deep shade of red when he nuzzled her curls before dragging his tongue along her slit and flicking it over her clit. No one had ever gone down on her before. She'd read about it in books. She'd heard other girls and women talk about it, but she'd never experienced it.

She was needy and panting when he lifted his face. "Think about me while I'm gone."

She nodded. How could she not?

He released her wrists to set his hands on her inner thighs and push them wide, his gaze lowering to her pussy. "I want to remove this hair," he stated, giving her curls a slight tug. "You can do it yourself or have Remi help you or I'll do it. Your choice."

She swallowed. Her entire body clenched when he was so bossy. He wasn't asking. He was telling her. She nodded. "Yes, Sir."

"There's hair remover in the packages. If you want to try

that, put a small amount on a spot first to make sure it doesn't burn your skin. Or you can use a razor. Or I'll be happy to set you on the counter in the bathroom, spread your legs open, and shave you myself if that's your preference."

She bit her lip, staring at him, wondering how he controlled her like this so easily. She would need to think about her options. Maybe she would ask Remi what Kade preferred. "Okay, Daddy."

He smiled. "Good girl." One more kiss to her pussy. "You'll stay in this room, right?"

She rolled her eyes. "You've told me like ten times. Besides I don't want anyone to know I'm here. They're going to be mad at me."

"No one is going to be mad at you after I talk to them, Baby girl. I promise. And don't be a sassy pants with Daddy. I'd hate to spank your naughty bottom twice in the same day."

She squirmed at the idea. She wasn't entirely opposed, and that embarrassed her.

"Okay." He stood again. "I'll be back as soon as I can."

Carlee pushed to sitting, tugging the shirt over her private parts just in case anyone was in the hallway when he opened the door. A lot of club members were pretty open about sex. She'd seen over half of them naked or partially naked over the years, but she'd never felt like the kind of person who'd want everyone in a room to see her naked body. Nor could she imagine having public sex.

It wasn't her thing. She hoped Atlas wouldn't parade her around naked in front of the entire MC. It didn't seem his style, but she was just starting to reacquaint herself with him. Anything was possible.

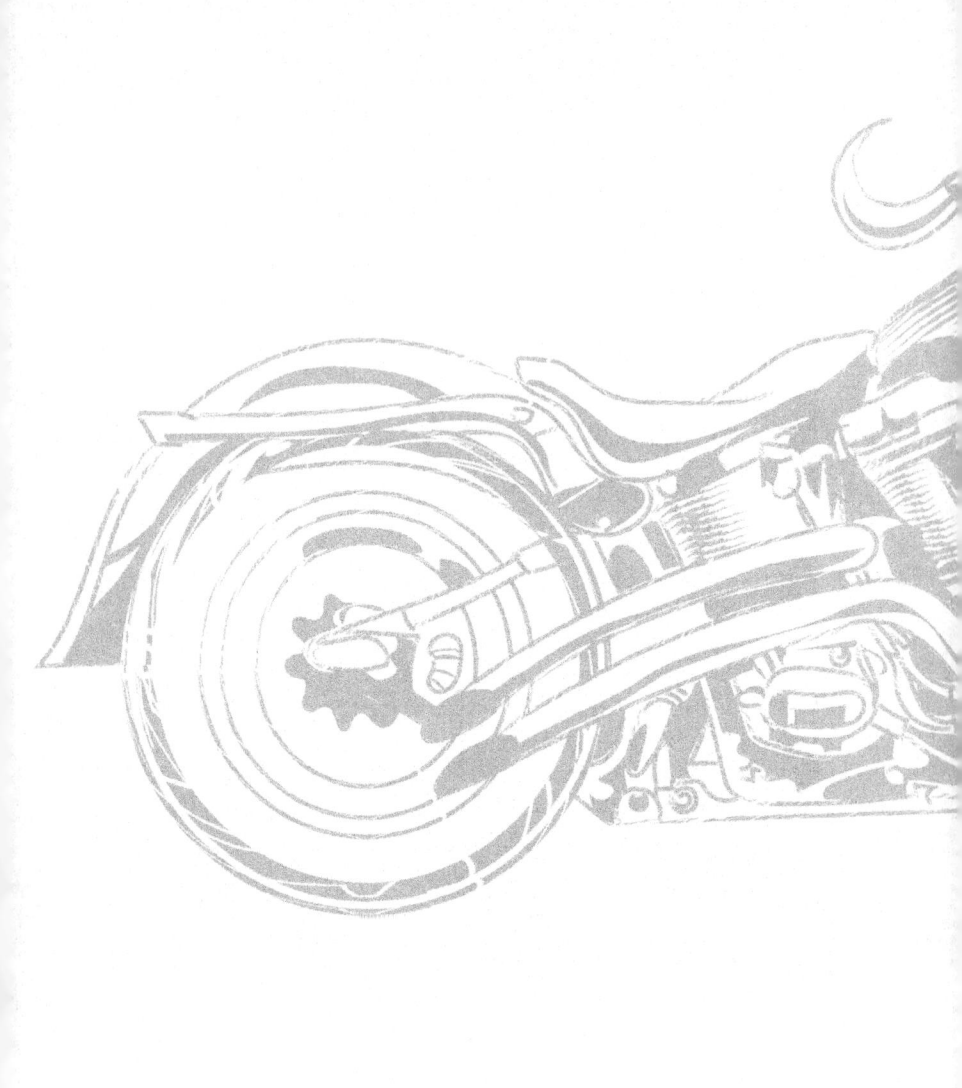

CHAPTER
NINE

When Atlas opened the door, he started laughing. He pushed it wider, and Remi came into view.

Remi took a step forward and gasped, her eyes wide. She glanced back and forth between Carlee and her brother. "It's Carlee?" She swatted playfully at his chest. "Why didn't you just tell me?"

He grabbed her hand. "It wasn't any of your business yet, nosy." He stepped to the side. "Carlee needs to talk to you. Please be nice."

Remi swatted at him again. "Since when have you known me to not be nice?"

"Extra nice then. And if you don't mind, keep her company for a few hours. I'll talk to Kade and tell him where you are. Don't leave my room."

"Why not?"

He narrowed his gaze at her. "Do you always question orders?"

She shrugged. "Usually." She squirmed next.

He chuckled. "Did you get your ass paddled this morning?"

"None of your business," she retorted before squeezing past him and shutting the door.

Carlee pulled her knees up to her chest as she watched her friend shuffle toward her. She wasn't sure where to start, but she decided to go with the obvious. "I'm sorry for my behavior for the past several months."

Remi came closer and climbed onto the bed. "It's okay. I'm sure you had your reasons. I wasn't a very good friend either. I've been so wrapped up in Kade that I didn't reach out to you as much as I should have. I was a bad friend. I'm sorry too."

"You have no reason to be sorry, but thank you." Carlee beamed at her. "Atlas told me you're with Kade."

Remi grinned. "Yeah. He's the best."

"I'm so happy for you."

Remi pointed at the pile of packages. "What's all this?"

Carlee smiled. "Christmas apparently. Atlas ordered it. I have no idea what it all is. You can help me open everything."

Remi clapped her hands together. "How fun." She tucked her dark hair behind her ear and licked the edge of her black-painted lips. "So... You and my brother?"

Carlee shrugged. "He says so, but he hasn't addressed the detail of him leaving. He's only here for a month. I need to guard my heart carefully."

Remi took her hand. "Why do I suspect it's already too late for that?"

Carlee sighed. "You're probably right."

"Maybe he wants to take you with him?"

Carlee shrugged again. "I don't belong in the city. This is my home."

"Well, we don't have to worry about it today. Let's dig into these packages." She nearly bounced.

"Do you want me to tell you about the last few months first?"

"Nope. You can tell me after." Remi grinned, her white teeth in stark contrast to her black lipstick. The perfect dark liner around her eyes was stunning on her. It had never been Carlee's style, but she'd always thought Remi pulled off the Goth look more than anyone she knew.

Carlee was relieved her best friend didn't seem angry. This wasn't going to go as badly as Carlee had pictured.

Remi held up a random package. "This one. Do this one first."

Carlee giggled as she rose onto her knees, nearly bouncing as she took it. "Are you going to help?"

"No. It's your Christmas. Not mine. I'm going to throw the wrapping on the floor and make a mess while you open everything." She covered her mouth in a giggle.

A giant weight lifted off Carlee's shoulders as she ripped open the first package and pulled out the cutest dress she'd ever seen. She held it up. It was something a toddler would wear. Pastel pink cotton with bunny ears, whiskers, eyes, and a cute little nose on the front.

"Oh, man. My brother has great taste. That's sooo you. It's adorable."

Carlee was embarrassed for half a second, and then she realized there was no reason to be. This was Remi. Her bestie. Carlee shouldn't care if Remi saw what was in all these packages. After all, most of them were sure to be clothes for a Little girl. Remi would eventually see them on Carlee anyway.

Carlee pulled the dress toward her chest, fighting back tears. She'd cried enough for a year today already. This time she was happy though. Happy and worried at the same time. What if Atlas showered her with presents for the next month and then left her? She would be devastated. Did he think she would eventually decide she could go back with him to the city?

Could she?

"Hey, don't cry," Remi encouraged. "Open another one." She handed Carlee a second package.

Carlee sucked back the tears, set the dress next to her, and opened the second bag. Her cheeks turned pink as she pulled out a package of cotton panties. Six in every color of pastel with little bows on the front. Full-cut briefs.

"Also your style. How does my brother know you so well?" Remi asked.

Carlee shrugged. "I don't know."

"Hey, was that your laundry he was doing in the middle of the night?" Remi asked.

"Yeah. I didn't have clean clothes."

"Did you even have any Little clothes?"

Carlee shook her head. "No. I've never had many Little things."

"Then I guess he went crazy." Remi bounced. "I'll tell you a secret that will make you laugh."

Carlee forced a smile. "What?"

Remi lowered her voice and glanced around as if anyone could hear them. "My Little loves pink. Kade buys me all kinds of frilly pink things. You probably won't even recognize me when you see me the first time super Little and pink."

Carlee giggled. "I can't wait."

Remi handed her the next package. "Another one."

For the next half hour, Carlee opened packages and Remi oohed and aahed over the contents. It was truly like the best Christmas and birthday combined.

Most of the gifts were clothes. One had a variety of hair clips, scrunchies, and bands in pastel colors. Two packages had shoes—a new pair of pink tennis shoes and a pair of pink ballet flats. There was girlie shampoo, conditioner, and body wash as well as bubble bath. Dolls and bath toys. The last package had the hair remover and razors Carlee had almost forgotten about.

Remi giggled. "I guess he's trying to tell you something."

Carlee stared at the package. "He warned me ahead of time about this one. He told me to either shave, have you do it, or he would do it."

Remi held her hands up. "I'm not doing it. I'd be afraid I'd cut my best friend."

"Do you do it yourself?"

Remi shook her head, her hair bouncing. "Not anymore. Kade does it." She covered her ears and squeezed her eyes closed. "I can tolerate a lot of things, but I can't picture my brother shaving my friend's pussy. Let's change the subject." She opened one eye a tiny slit.

Carlee giggled. "Okay. Fine."

Remi shoved the last of the paper to the floor and crawled up to lean against the headboard next to Carlee. "Now. Tell me everything."

CHAPTER
TEN

Atlas hesitated for a moment when he entered the room a few hours later. Packing materials were strewn all over the floor, the bed was covered with the contents, and his chest tightened when he realized Carlee was nowhere in sight.

It only took him a moment to notice the bathroom door was closed and light was coming out from under it.

As he crossed the room toward the bathroom, he paused when he heard voices. Maybe Remi was in there with Carlee. Except he'd seen Remi leaving the compound with Kade ten minutes ago. She wasn't in the attached bathroom.

Atlas knocked softly on the door. "Carlee?"

"Atlas?"

"Yes, Baby girl. Who else would be out here? May I come in?"

"Yeah."

He opened the door slowly and looked around. She was in the bathtub. Alone. The water was high. Bubbles were so out of control they were spilling over the top. Her hair was wet. Her cheeks were pink.

He furrowed his brows. "Who were you talking to, Baby girl?"

Her hands were under the water, and she slowly lifted them, revealing two mermaid Barbies. "They were trying to decide where to go to dinner on girls' night out," she informed him softly.

His heart clenched so tight. He didn't think he'd ever seen or heard anything sweeter in his life. The only thing wrong with this picture was that he'd rather give her a bath himself.

He stepped in farther and leaned against the vanity. "You're all wrinkly like a prune. How long have you been in there?"

She shrugged adorably. "I dunno." She tipped her head back and met his gaze. "Did I do something naughty?"

"No, Baby girl. Not at all." He squatted down next to her and tucked a wet curl behind her ear. "In the future, I'd rather bathe you myself, but you didn't know that, and I'm glad you found something to entertain yourself."

She glanced past him toward the vanity. "I was going to shave, but I got too scared. Remi said Kade does it for her. Can you do it?"

"Of course, Little one. I'd be happy to." He shoved a pile of bubbles toward her. "Looks like someone added a bit too many bubbles to the tub."

"I didn't know they would grow this big. I haven't ever had bubbles before. Are you mad?"

He frowned. "No, Carlee. Daddy is not mad. Not about anything. Or...did you want me to be mad?"

She shook her head. "No. Of course not. Why would I want you to be mad?" She trailed one of the mermaids' tails through the bubbles, not meeting his eyes.

"Mmm. Maybe because your spanking wore off, and you're hoping I'll swat your little bottom again. Is that possible?"

She shrugged. "No."

Atlas tipped her chin back. "Listen to Daddy, Baby girl.

Our relationship is new, and we'll be feeling each other out for a long time. But my responses and reactions will eventually become predictable. You need to know that I will never be mad at you. I won't ever punish you because I'm angry. That's not how a good Daddy operates."

"But you spanked me this morning when I was naughty," she pointed out, confusion etched on her pretty face.

He smiled. "I wasn't angry. There's a difference. Sometimes you'll need to be disciplined for being sassy or breaking a rule, but I will never be mad." He leaned closer, wanting to be sure she fully understood the next part. "Sometimes you might need Daddy to spank your bottom just because. That's okay too. You don't have to intentionally be naughty to get your bottom swatted. You could just ask Daddy to do it if you feel like you need the release."

"Oh." She lifted her two dolls again and helped them float in the water as the bubbles continued to pop.

Atlas watched her play until she started shivering as the water grew too cool. "Ready to get out?"

She shrugged. "You're going to shave me," she murmured.

"Yes. And then I'm going to rub my beard against your smooth skin and suckle your soft pussy until you scream like you did this morning."

Her eyes were wide as saucers. "No one's ever done that to me before."

He smiled so broadly his cheeks hurt. "I'm glad. I like knowing I'm the only man who's made you come or gone down on you."

"You make me feel totally out of control."

"That's the goal." She was so fucking cute.

Finally, she set her mermaids on the corner of the tub. "I think I'm ready to get out now, Daddy."

He lowered his hand down into the water and pulled out the stopper before reaching under her arms and lifting her out of the water. He stood her on the bath mat and grabbed a towel to dry her off from head to toe.

When he was done, he folded the towel in half, set it on the vanity, and lifted her up to sit on it. "Lean back and spread your legs wide for Daddy."

She bit her bottom lip as she opened herself up to him. "Everything is so much more intense with you."

He shot her a grin while he squirted shaving cream on her mound. "Daddies can be intense."

"You won't cut me?"

"Nope. I'll be very careful." And as difficult as it was to shave his precious Little girl's pussy without having an orgasm in his jeans, he somehow managed, concentrating on her folds, taking his time to drag the razor over every inch of her skin until she was smooth. "There."

Her face was beet red. "You're done?"

"I'm done." He wiped the last of the shaving cream away, opened a drawer, and grabbed a handheld mirror. Angling it between her legs, he showed her. "See? Not a single cut."

She reached between her legs with one hand and dragged her fingers over her smooth pussy. "It's weird."

"It won't seem weird for very long. You'll like it. I've heard some women who keep their pussies bare feel more aroused all the time from the sensitive skin against their panties."

She lowered her legs. "Can I have some panties now?"

He shook his head and lifted her to her feet. "No. You can have my mouth on you now." He patted her bottom. "But first, I'm going to comb through your hair and get all the tangles out."

She sighed, which pleased him. She was anxious to move to the part where he suckled her pussy. That was a good sign. He was glad she'd had only unmemorable, poorly executed sexual experiences with Silver, and apparently every other man she'd been with.

Even though she wasn't a virgin, in a lot of ways she was.

Her first orgasm in front of someone was his. Her first orgasm against a man's mouth was about to be his. Her first orgasm with a cock buried in her would also be his. Tonight? Maybe. He wasn't sure. He would play that by ear. If she didn't seem ready to take that step with him, he would wait.

Atlas combed out her hair and then took her hand and led her to the bedroom. He lifted her onto the bed before tugging his T-shirt over his head. He left his jeans on for now, but kicked off his shoes.

Her breath hitched as she scanned his chest. "How does an accountant get so muscular?"

He scooted her back, chuckling. "Accountants are allowed to go to the gym, you know."

She giggled as she set her palms on his pecs and smoothed them down his body. "Are you going to have sex with me?"

"If it's what you want. I won't rush you." He nestled between her legs and lowered his face to her breasts, suckling first one nipple and then the other back and forth until they were both hard peaks and she was writhing beneath him.

He slid farther down her body, held her thighs open, and lowered his mouth to her smooth pussy.

Carlee arched her hips off the bed when he rubbed his bearded cheek against her soft mound. She smelled so good and the wetness leaking out of her called to him.

He thrust his tongue into her tight channel before lapping at her clit.

Carlee grabbed his shoulders and held on while he suckled, licked, and flicked her swollen nub.

"Oh, God," she moaned. "I'm gonna come."

He chuckled against her skin. "That is the idea, Baby girl."

"Please…" She fisted the sheets at her sides, arching and squirming.

He'd never seen anyone sexier in his life. No one had ever gotten under his skin and made him want to worship their body for the rest of his days. There'd never been a single woman he'd wanted to bury his cock in more than Carlee Deveraux.

Capturing her clit between his teeth, he flicked the little nub over and over until she stiffened and screamed. And the words she screamed warmed his heart. "Atlas... Daddy..." Music. Perfection.

When he finally lifted his head, rose up a few inches, and looked down, he found his cock was so engorged the tip was sticking out of the top of his jeans.

Carlee was panting as she grabbed his biceps. "Please, Daddy. I need you."

He slid off the bed and popped the button on his jeans. "You need my cock, Baby girl?"

She nodded vigorously. "Yes, Daddy. Please. Don't tease me. I want to feel you inside me."

Atlas shrugged out of his jeans as fast as he could, snagged a condom from the drawer on the nightstand, and rolled it on in record time.

Carlee had let her legs remain wide open, her glistening pussy calling to him. She was breathing heavily. Her hair was damp and spread out over the pillow.

Gorgeous. Intoxicating. She was his life. It didn't matter that she didn't fully believe him yet. He would convince her. Once he'd been inside her body, they would be even more bonded.

He slowly crawled between her legs, his heavy cock bobbing.

She stared down at it, panting. "Uhh..."

That was all he needed to hear to get a big head. Apparently Silver and any other man before him had had a tiny dick. Good. He would erase her memory of any previous man in about five seconds.

Dropping down over her, he lined his cock up with her entrance and cupped her face. He took her lips in a deep passionate kiss, wanting her to be soft and pliable before he entered her.

Her hands came to his hips before she dug her fingers into his ass. She moaned into his mouth, her tongue eagerly dueling with his.

When she grew restless beneath him, he released her lips, held her gaze, and eased into her. Her lips parted, her eyes rolled back, and the sweetest deep moan filled the room.

God, he loved the way her fingers gripped his ass. He loved the way she arched her tits so they rubbed against his chest. He loved the way her face settled into a blissful state, her mouth turned up in a smile, her button nose flaring, her eyes moving rapidly behind her nearly closed lids.

He loved… Jesus, he loved her. This woman he'd known since she was a small child. This woman who slammed into his heart like a freight train less than twenty-four hours ago. A gorgeous, sexy, Little girl who was trusting him with her heart, her safety, and her soul.

He gritted his teeth as he filled her. She was so fucking tight, and it had been a long time since he'd been inside a woman. Plus, no experience had ever been as important as this one. Carlee was his life. His world. His heart.

She was his in every way. Life would sort itself out. It had to. There were no other options.

"Atlas…" His name on her lips as he bottomed out was music. Heavenly music.

He held steady, grinding the base of his cock against her clit until she bucked and whimpered.

The world stopped spinning. It was just the two of them. Nothing else existed. This blissful happiness. Perfection. A moment in time he would use to mark everything before and everything after. Before Carlee there had not been as many colors or sounds or scents.

The world would be brighter and happier and so much more

when they woke up tomorrow. They had a lot of shit to deal with, but he would ignore it until tomorrow. Now was for Carlee. Now was for his Little girl. The woman who held his heart in her palm.

He eased partway out and then back in. Deeper. So fucking good. So perfect. She was meant for him. Her body molded to his as if she were born to envelop him.

He wished he could make this last longer than it was going to, but there was no helping the fact that his cock was about to explode from past neglect and current perfection.

She gasped several times, her grip tightening on his butt cheeks, her mouth open. And then she came, shuddering violently as her channel gripped his cock so tight she might strangle him.

He couldn't hold back any longer. He let himself go on the heels of her orgasm, pulse after pulse of his release filling the condom as if it weren't big enough to contain him.

When he was finally spent, his arms were trembling, but he didn't want to pull out of her yet. He wanted to savor this moment. He kissed her gently, loving the way she smiled against his lips without returning the kiss.

Finally, she blinked and grinned at him. "How do you have the brainpower to tell your lips what to do?"

He chuckled, a deep sound that vibrated through both of them. He kissed her again. "You're mine, Carlee Marie," he reminded her. He would do so often. Until she believed him. Until she looked him in the eye and showed him she accepted the declaration completely.

He would know. It would shine in her eyes. Right now, she was still skeptical. He had to accept that. It changed nothing. Rushing her wasn't necessary. She would catch up. She had to. They'd only been together less than a day as a couple.

Tonight he would sleep under the covers. Both of them naked. He would hold her in his arms all night tonight and every single night for the rest of their lives.

There was no other option.

CHAPTER
ELEVEN

Carlee woke up to the sun streaming far too bright into the room. She was confused for only a moment before she remembered where she was and who she was with.

He was still wrapped around her, spooning her from behind in the same position he'd pulled her into when he'd declared they were going to sleep.

She hadn't felt this well-rested in…forever. A comfortable warm bed. Nice clean sheets. No neighbors yelling at each other through thin walls. A room that was the right temperature instead of always too hot or too cold.

And Atlas. Her Daddy. He held her like she was the most precious thing in his world. He made her feel that way too. All the time. In everything he did. He was rock solid in his belief she was his.

She trusted him. She did. She wanted to believe this fairy tale could be real and lasting, but it was so hard.

Atlas had worked hard to get out of this town and move to the big city. He'd been a brainiac in high school and a model student who got a great scholarship, graduated college with honors, and took a job with a big accounting firm.

Yeah, he had some tattoos he easily hid under long-sleeved shirts. Yeah, he was a Daddy deep down that either came from instinct or his upbringing. And yes, he clearly loved his Harley.

On the flip side, he also pulled off a clean-cut guy. He had short-cropped hair, a groomed beard, perfectly straight teeth, deep blue eyes, and a smile that probably made women swoon. Why was he single?

Suddenly, his arms snaked tighter around her and he held her closer, his lips coming to her ear. "What's going through that pretty head, Baby girl?"

"Why don't you have a girlfriend?" she blurted out.

"I *do*."

She stiffened, nearly jumping out of her skin so fast her head was spinning. She twisted around and glared at him, scrambling to get free of him and the covers, batting at him with both hands so he would let her go.

He started chuckling, which only infuriated her further. "Let me go. Why are you laughing? This isn't funny. I don't date other people's boyfriends." Her voice rose to a shrill sound.

Atlas grabbed her wrists, flattened her to her back, and pinned her arms above her head. When she still fought him, so furious now she could scream, he pinned her body down with a leg over her torso.

She was naked and fuming angry. "Get off me!"

He was laughing. Damn him. "Carlee Marie, stop fighting me and look at me."

She jerked her head all the way to the side so she wouldn't have to see his face, feeling very defiant.

He kissed her neck. Damn infuriating man. Why would he think she would have consented to dating someone else's boyfriend? She'd known he would break her heart when he left town to go back to his real life, but she hadn't expected him to hurt her this badly on day two.

"Are you done having your little tantrum, Baby girl?" he asked calmly, his voice still filled with laughter.

"No."

"Okay. That's fine. After I explain myself, I will flip you over and spank your cute little bottom until you can't sit for the rest of the day. Then you can stand in the corner for a while with your red-hot bottom on display for me."

She tried to squirm free, but he outweighed her by at least double, plus he was strong and fit. She secretly vowed to start hitting the gym…as soon as she got a new job and made enough money to afford a new car, a new apartment, and a new life. No thanks to Atlas.

"You can't spank me. And I don't date other people's boyfriends. Go back to the big city and spank your girlfriend," she taunted.

His body shook as he laughed some more.

She growled. This was so not funny. She was not going to look at him though. No way. She twisted her head farther away, nearly craning her neck to avoid even seeing him out of her peripheral vision.

Why did he have to be so fucking gorgeous and sexy? If she saw even his ear, she would cave. He had that effect on her.

"First of all," he began as if any explanation would make her stop seeing red, "I told you we are not dating. Stop saying that. We were never dating. I claimed your sweet and sassy Little the moment I saw you. You're mine. If you need me to, I'll toss you over my shoulder, drag you to the courthouse today, and make you my wife so you'll stop thinking I'm not serious."

She couldn't believe him. She jerked her head around—even though it was the last thing she'd wanted to do—and glared at him hard. "What is your girlfriend going to think if you get married while you're here?"

He smirked. "I don't know. You tell me." He lifted a brow.

"How the hell should I know?" she shouted. "Why don't you call her and ask her and while you're at it, you can—" Carlee's heart stopped as realization dawned. She clamped her mouth shut as her face heated. *Shit. Fuck. Damn.*

Atlas started laughing. "She's catching on."

"*I'm* your girlfriend..." she murmured.

He smiled broadly.

Her face heated further. "Why did you let me carry on like that?"

More laughter. "You haven't given me a single moment to respond, Baby girl. You went into full defense mode in point five seconds. You asked if I had a girlfriend, and I answered truthfully. But I'm not really fond of having a girlfriend. I'm kind of liking the courthouse idea more by the second. I think after I spank your adorable bottom, I'll stand you in the corner and use the time to look online at rings and the courthouse hours."

She gasped. He couldn't be serious. "You can't do that."

"Why not?"

"For about ten reasons." She tugged to get her arms free, but he wouldn't let go. If anything, he held her tighter, his thigh pinning her torso to the bed.

"List them."

Her chest heaved. Her breasts rising and falling.

"Go ahead. List the reasons why I can't marry you."

"For one we haven't even been *dating* for a full day," she countered, tossing that word out again.

He shook his head. "We aren't dating now either, *girlfriend*. We are in a solid committed relationship," Atlas declared.

Her eyes bulged. "That's crazy. It's not possible."

"Have you been cheating on me?" he teased.

"I haven't even left the room since you dragged me here against my will," she retorted.

He chuckled. "Carlee, you are not here against your will.

You got on my bike all by yourself. I didn't even have to count to three or throw you over my shoulder."

"You coerced me," she yelled. She hoped the walls really were as insulated as she'd always been told. She sure didn't want anyone in the MC to overhear this. She wasn't even ready for anyone to know she was in the building let alone hear her discussing this absurd marriage idea.

"I threatened to spank you, which you secretly craved, so it wasn't really coercion. We are the perfect definition of a solid committed relationship. We are exclusive. We respect each other. We put each other first. We're living together. We want the same things. Committed. Give me another argument. That one is weak."

"Fine. We don't live in the same town." She came super close to sticking her tongue out at him but decided it wasn't in her best interest. Besides she was trying to be an adult here, not a sassy girl.

"We will never be separated even for a night starting yesterday. I don't care if that's here or there or out in the ocean on a dinghy. Next concern?"

"You can't know me well enough to make that kind of commitment, Atlas." She was grasping at straws. How was he able to break down all her arguments?

"I've known you since you were five. I know you better than anyone alive. I know things about you most people will never know. Furthermore, you know me even better than I know you because I'm embarrassed to say I wasn't paying as close attention to you at fifteen as you were to me. Granted, if I had been, I might have ended up breaking a few laws, so it was probably for the best. But you've thought about me for a long time. Am I lacking in any way you were hoping for?" He was half teasing. She could hear it in his voice.

"Don't be ridiculous. You're ten times more than I could ever have hoped for," she blurted before realizing she was showing her cards and clamping her lips shut.

She decided to deflect that last part. "And what do you know about me that no one else knows?"

"I know you and Remi snuck out at night most weekends during your freshman year of high school to go to parties with older boys."

She gasped. "How did you know that?"

His deep chuckle shook her frame again. "I saw you when I visited. I followed the two of you several times to make sure you were safe."

"So while I was flirting with older boys who were maybe seventeen or eighteen, my best friend's twenty-three-year-old brother was perving on us?"

He laughed hard. "I was never perving on my sister. I was making sure you were safe. And I got close enough several times to notice you personally never flirted with anyone. Usually you pulled a book out of your bag, curled up in a corner, and read while Remi was partying and dancing."

Carlee was so stunned she couldn't respond.

"I also know you and Remi were the ones who tried to make coffee in the middle of the night when you were about twelve. You forgot the pot and it ran all over the floor and the two of you scurried from the room and left that giant mess for Dad to find in the morning."

Carlee's mouth fell open. "You took the blame for that."

"Yep. Dad would have been furious if he thought you two were making coffee. I told him I was so tired from studying over my break that I forgot the pot and even that I'd made the coffee at all and fell asleep waiting for it."

"I can't believe you did that."

"Why were you making coffee anyway?" he asked.

"We wanted to know what it tasted like. No one would let us have any."

"Did you ever start drinking coffee, Baby girl?" His voice softened, and he kissed her chest between her breasts.

"No," she murmured. "It's yucky."

His smile lit up the room. "Good. It's not good for you. I won't be filling your sippy cups with coffee." He nuzzled her neck. "Do you have any other arguments for why we can't get married before I spank your naughty bottom?"

"You haven't asked me," she pointed out.

"Mmm. True. Shall I do that now?"

She shook her head, giggling. "No, Daddy. Not now. Not naked while you're pinning me to the bed about to spank me. It should be special."

Another heart-stopping smile spread across his face. "Okay, Baby girl. I'll come up with something special. I promise. But stop this nonsense about dating and girlfriends and living arrangements. You're my girlfriend. You'll soon be my fiancée for about ten seconds. And then you'll be my wife. The rest will fall into place. I promise. My top priority for the rest of my life is you. Always you. Your welfare and health and safety. Making sure you know you are loved. Making you squirm and scream when I suck your little pussy. Wiping away your tears after you purge icky feelings with a spanking. Nothing else will ever be more important to me than you."

Atlas lowered his lips to hers and kissed her gently, melting her insides to a pile of goo.

When he finally released her wrists and lifted his leg, he flipped her over onto her tummy without a word. "I get the feeling my Baby girl is going to need a daily maintenance spanking to remember how much I adore her."

Carlee whimpered as she tucked her hands under her chest. "I don't need a spanking," she lied.

He kissed the small of her back and trailed his fingers over her bottom. "Liar. Liars get even more swats."

Goosebumps rose all over her skin.

"Spread your legs, Baby girl. Naughty girls don't get orgasms with their spankings."

She pouted as she parted her thighs. Darn. She could really

use an orgasm right about now instead of a spanking. But she'd dug this hole herself.

Atlas sat up next to her, seemingly completely unbothered by his nudity and his semihard cock. He set one hand on her lower back and swatted her bottom with the other palm.

She flinched. He didn't spend as much time warming her up and preparing her as yesterday. She wasn't a newbie anymore. Soon he was spanking her harder, the heat spreading all over her bottom and thighs as she sank into the mattress and buried her face in the pillow.

She wasn't as stiff this time. She absorbed the swats, let her mind relax, and enjoyed every moment of his attention. It felt so good. Who knew she would have a spanking fetish? And maybe she wouldn't have with the wrong man. The wrong Daddy. She certainly wouldn't have let Silver spank her. Never. Not a chance in hell. But Atlas... Every swat was delicious.

She knew he was watching her closely, but he didn't stop this time to check in over and over. He undoubtedly read her body language, the moans and whimpers. The way she arched her hips off the bed into his palm would be all the information he needed.

When the burning sensation switched to a hot sting, her tears fell. Sobbing started. He only spanked her a few more times before he stopped, gathered her gently in his arms, and held her close.

He kissed all over her face. "Such a good girl. Let it all out."

She cried. Damn him for being right about everything. It felt so good to have her naughty behavior purged with his palm and then her tears. "I'm sorry, D-D-Daddy," she choked out. "I won't doubt you like that again."

He kissed her cheeks and wiped her tears. "You'll probably have a few more doubts, Baby girl. Daddy understands. I swooped into town and claimed you as my Little girl so fast you never saw me coming. It's only fair to expect you to have concerns. Eventually you'll see and believe you are mine."

She hiccupped a few times, embarrassed that he kept seeing this side of her. She'd cried so many times in the last day and a half that he must think it was all she ever did. "I'm sorry." She tried to wipe the tears and suck them back. Who wanted to date a girl who was so emotional?

He reached over to the nightstand and snagged a pile of tissues, which he held up to her nose. "Blow, Baby girl."

When she tried to take them from him and do it herself, he snagged her wrist and held her hand in her lap. "Blow, Carlee."

So she did. She let this amazing Daddy wipe her nose and her tears.

Afterward, he took her chin. "Now, I don't want you to ever apologize for crying, got it? Little girls cry sometimes. You're having big feelings right now. You've been through a lot in the past several months. There's nothing wrong with needing to let it out."

She sniffled. "You don't want a whiny brat crying on your lap every day," she argued.

"You are not a whiny brat. A sassy pants sometimes, but not a brat and certainly not whiny. Your tears are legit. I'm humbled and so glad to be here to spank you when you need the outlet and hold you afterward. You'll feel much better after a firm spanking and a good cry. Daddy never wants you to hold back."

She swallowed and nodded.

He rose from the bed and set her on her feet before pointing at the corner. "Go stand in that corner now, Baby girl."

She sighed. She wasn't interested in this part. Why did she need a timeout?

"Do you need me to count to three, Carlee?"

She sniffled again and stared at him. "Why do I need a timeout?"

"There are a number of reasons why I will put you in time-out, Little one. First of all, it gives you time to think about whatever got your bottom swatted in the first place. Today you can think about how to start trusting Daddy enough not to doubt me at every turn. Another reason for a timeout after a spanking is to help you get your arousal in check. After a hard spanking, you will usually feel aroused. Daddy will not reward you with an orgasm. You'll stand there with your legs parted until it subsides."

She flinched. How did he know? She eased her legs together, thinking to squeeze her thighs tight.

"Carlee…" he warned. "Do you need me to check how wet you are for myself to prove my point?"

She shook her head. "No, Daddy."

"I didn't think so. Now, go stand in the corner like a good girl before I decide to double your time."

She sighed as she shuffled in that direction. When she got to the corner, she wasn't sure what to do next.

"Spread your legs, toes on each wall. Lean your forehead into the corner. Clasp your hands at the small of your back."

She shuddered as she got into this humiliating position. She knew her bottom was bright red. It stung fiercely. Her legs shook. She felt very small and vulnerable. And wetness leaked down her legs. Dammit.

Atlas moved around the room. He even went into the bathroom and took a shower. She didn't dare move an inch while he did so. It didn't take him long. Soon he was back, opening drawers and moving the chair at the desk. Every sound was heightened.

When she couldn't hear him anymore, she assumed he was on his computer at the desk. She went into her head and thought about everything he'd said.

He really wanted to marry her? That seemed ludicrous. She was nobody.

She drew in a deep breath, imagining what he would say if she said that out loud. He would spank her again, harder, and leave her in this corner for the rest of the day probably.

But seriously, it was hard for her to wrap her mind around this total change in her circumstances, both physical and financial as well as the mere idea of having a Daddy. It had happened so fast her head was spinning.

He'd flippantly used the word love a few times too. Did he mean it? Did he love her? She couldn't marry him if he didn't love her like a man should love a woman. She didn't want to be just his Little girl. She wanted to be his lover in every way too.

She certainly had been last night when he'd made sweet love to her until the earth spun off its axis, showing her for the first time in her life what it meant to be cherished and adored.

Lord knew Carlee didn't have good examples or role models. Her own mother had gone through men like she went through packs of cigarettes. She hadn't loved any of them. She hadn't even loved Carlee. She'd simply bided her time until the child she'd unintentionally birthed had been old enough for her to skip town. And she'd never looked back.

It didn't hurt anymore. It hadn't even hurt then. Carlee had spent most of her time with the MC for most of her life by then anyway. She'd had other people who'd loved her. She'd often eaten at the Monroe house.

By the time Carlee was eighteen and her mother had disappeared, she'd been kind of relieved. She hadn't had to tiptoe around the trailer any longer, wondering if a strange man would be there to ogle her. She'd had the entire place to herself. She could tidy it up and no one would make a mess. She didn't have to deal with cigarettes or drug paraphernalia any longer.

Maybe she should feel guilty about not caring that her

mother had left her and never contacted her again. But she didn't. And she'd had people to rely on. Until six months ago when Silver had fucked with her life and made a mess of it.

After she'd left Silver, Carlee had told herself she would never put her trust in a man again. They were manipulative and mean. They only wanted her for cooking, cleaning, and fucking. The fucking wasn't even good, and she'd never been able to cook or clean to Silver's satisfaction.

And then Atlas showed up two nights ago and turned her world upside down. He wasn't like Silver or any other man she'd ever known. He was firm and demanding but in a kind and nurturing way.

Atlas didn't scare her. He didn't make demands she couldn't handle. He didn't boss her around in the same way Silver had. Not for his own gratification. He was bossy in a different way. He did it for her. He made demands he knew she needed and craved.

She took a deep breath and blew it out slowly.

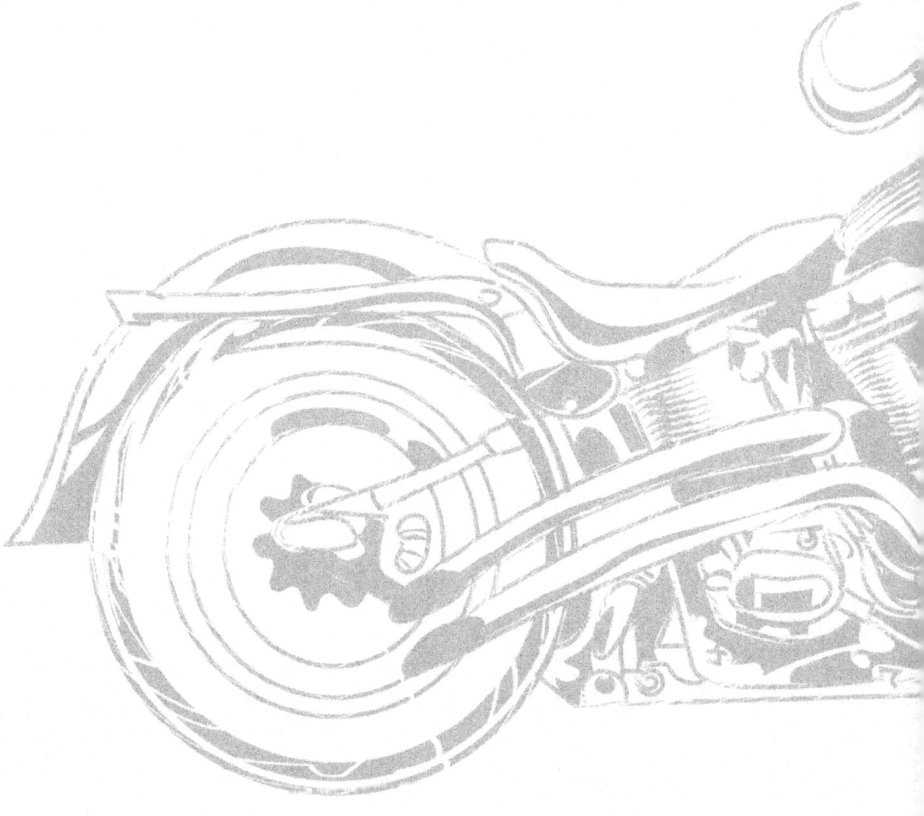

CHAPTER
TWELVE

"Okay, Baby girl. Your timeout is done. Come here." Atlas said this in a calm voice that made her insides tingly.

Carlee felt very Little and needy as she turned around and shuffled toward him. He was dressed. He had on jeans and a khaki long-sleeved Henley. His hair was damp but combed. He even had on his boots already.

She was nervous as she approached. His full attire made her feel self-conscious and small in her naked skin.

He reached out, picked her up by the hips, and settled her on his lap. After tipping her chin back, he met her gaze. "You okay, Baby girl?"

She nodded. "I'm sorry for not believing in you and being sassy, Daddy."

He kissed her nose.

"I promise I will be a good housekeeper and I'll learn to cook meals you like too." She didn't know why she felt the need to blurt that out. It just happened.

He frowned. "What are you talking about, Little one?"

She looked around. "Wherever we live, I mean. Or even

here. I left a mess yesterday all over the floor and the bed. You cleaned it up. I should have done that."

His frown deepened. "Daddy might have some rules about keeping your playroom clean or putting your dishes in the sink, Baby girl, but you won't be cooking and cleaning for me. Why would you think that?" His eyes widened. "Oh... Silver treated you like a domestic slave, didn't he?"

Her cheeks heated as she nodded.

"He wasn't a Daddy at all, Carlee. He was an abuser. You're not my slave. You're my Little girl. I'll be taking care of you, not the other way around. It's in my blood. It's why I'm a Daddy. I have a deep need to be the nurturer. It pleases me greatly when you let me take care of you. I loved that you ripped into all those packages and left a mess. It looked like happiness and smiles happened in here." He smiled and tickled her tummy.

She giggled. "It did?"

"Yes. And Little girls don't cook. Not mine anyway. Daddy will do the cooking. You may watch or set the table. If you want to help sometimes, I'll give you jobs that don't involve knives or flames or the oven."

"Really?" She struggled to believe this could be true. It was like all the books she'd ever read about Daddies combined in this one perfect Daddy. She'd never expected to find out or meet one or have one. She thought they were just fictional.

"Definitely. Have you seen Little girls running around the clubhouse cleaning, Carlee?"

She thought about it and shook her head. "No."

"Other MCs might look drastically different from this one. MCs where most of the members aren't Daddies. But the Shadowridge Guardians are just that, guardians. Protectors. Nurturers. We can cook and clean and chase Little girls around all day. Like me, it's in their blood."

"I haven't had a chance to really talk to Remi about her

relationship with Kade since I wasn't here when they started seeing each other."

"Well, I know Kade, and I'm certain Remi is not his domestic servant," Atlas informed her. He patted her knees. "Now, I need you to be brave for me today. I want you to leave the room. Not the compound or even the building. Just the room. Can you do that?"

She stared at him, heart racing. "People will be mad at me."

He shook his head. "No, they won't. If anyone even looks at you sideways, Daddy will handle them. But I've already met with the principal officers yesterday and set them straight on what happened with Silver. I don't want you to feel like you have to hide in here all the time. That's over. Plus, I have to work in the treasurer's office, and I want you where I can see you, not alone in this room."

She drew in a brave breath. "Okay, Daddy." She glanced down. "I might need clothes."

He tickled her tummy again. "Sassy pants." After standing her on her feet in front of him, he strode to the dresser, opened a few drawers, and returned with several items of clothing. Not the clothes she'd come here with but the ones he'd bought her yesterday.

Daddy held up the pretty pink bunny dress first. "Do you like this?"

She nodded rapidly before slowing her nod and glancing at the door. "But is it appropriate to wear out of the room?"

He draped the dress over the open laptop on his desk, sat, and held up a pair of pink panties. "Hold my shoulders and step in."

She grabbed onto him and chewed on her bottom lip while she let this surreal experience happen. This man was her Daddy and he was dressing her? She needed to pinch herself.

"Arms up," he insisted next. He pulled the dress over her head when she complied. When he smoothed the cotton down, he patted her bottom. "You're totally covered. What's wrong with wearing it outside the room?"

"I look..."

"Little?" He chuckled.

"Well, yeah."

"And have you never seen any other Little girls in this MC?"

She sighed. "Of course I have, but no one has seen *me* this way before. They might stare."

"They might do a doubletake, but they'll get over it fast. They'll be pleased to find out you've found a Daddy, a real one. They'll also be too busy hoping this means I'm going to stay." He wiggled his brows.

She tipped her head back. "Does it mean that?"

He pulled her between his legs and cupped her face. "I don't know yet, Baby girl. I haven't had time to think about anything except making sure you're safe and know that you're mine. That's been ninety percent of my focus. The other ten percent has been figuring out what the fuck Silver was doing before he took off."

He stroked her head. "Can you live with that for now, Baby girl?"

She nodded. "Yes, Daddy."

"Good. Now, let's get your shoes and socks on, then Daddy will fix your hair, then we'll head to the kitchen. You need to eat."

"Okay, Daddy." She didn't argue with him as he led her to the bed, set her on the edge, and put frilly white folded socks on before her new pink tennis shoes. She didn't say a word as he led her to the bathroom, carefully parted her hair, and arranged two high pigtails, including pink ribbons.

She couldn't say anything during all of that because she was too choked up. If she'd tried to speak, she would have cried. She didn't want to cry again this morning. She might have been Little and sliding into a far more comfortable headspace, but she was still fierce inside, and she didn't want to get all sobby and keep Atlas from doing his work.

As he finished with her hair, he stood behind her and looked at her in the mirror. "Did I do a good job?"

She nodded. "Better than I usually do." She glanced down at the hard points of her nipples, so obvious against the front of the cotton dress. "People are going to see my nipples."

"Everyone has nipples. I don't think anyone will be shocked to find out you do too," he teased.

She rolled her eyes. "Daddy…"

He rounded to the front of her and met her gaze, his hands on her shoulders. "When we're inside the compound, I want you to be free to be yourself. Little. My Little girl. There might be a few Littles who wear bras around here, but it's not the norm, is it?"

She nodded slowly. "No, Sir."

"I bet you feel more in your Little headspace without a bra on." He lifted a brow.

"Yeah."

"I will not expose you to anyone without your permission. We can discuss how comfortable you are about getting spanked in front of people another time. You probably don't know yet what aspects of spanking you'd like to keep private. Some Little girls like to be reprimanded in public. Some are titillated by having their panties pulled down and their bare bottoms swatted in front of people. They enjoy the humiliation. But you're not ready to know that about yourself yet, and I'm not ready to know if I'm willing to expose your bottom and pussy to other people either, to be honest. But I certainly won't take your shirt or dress off in front of people ever. They might see your hard little buds through the front of your dresses, but that's all." He slid his hands down and flicked his thumbs over the tips, making them even harder.

She wiggled. "Daddy…"

"We good?"

She drew in a breath. "Yes, Sir."

He pulled her in for a hug and kissed the top of her head.

When he led her back to the bedroom, he pointed at his laptop. "I picked out several rings I thought would look pretty on you, Baby girl."

She gasped. "You really did that?"

"I said I would."

"But…"

He kissed her forehead. "No buts. Just Daddy looking at rings. Do you want to see them?"

She shook her head so her pigtails went flying.

"Why not?"

"Because…" How should she say this?

"Be honest."

"Because I don't want to see the ring you buy me. I want it to be a surprise. I'll love it no matter what. Also, I don't want to know when you bought it. And also…"

He grinned. "Go on."

"That's a bit too real for me to trust or wrap my head around, Daddy."

He kissed her lips. "Thanks for being honest."

When he opened the door, she held her breath. This was a big deal to her. He might have met with a few key members of the MC last night, but most members wouldn't have found out she was in the compound, and she wasn't sure how many would be on Silver's side of things.

As soon as they stepped into the hallway, they ran into Steele and Ivy. Ivy rushed forward and gave Carlee a hug. "Hey, Carlee. Daddy told me what happened with Silver. I'm so sorry none of us knew and no one worked harder to help you. I feel bad."

Carlee hugged her back, quickly realizing her promise not to cry was going to get obliterated. "Thank you," was all she could manage to murmur and still hold back the tears.

Ivy took her hand. "I was just going to get breakfast. Wanna come with me?"

"What are you doing up and running so early?" Atlas asked Steele.

"I thought it prudent that I help you in any way I can. I didn't realize until Silver vanished that the books were such a mess or that something nefarious might have happened. Plus, Ivy was bouncing off the walls of our apartment, wanting to see Carlee."

Carlee glanced at Steele's firm expression before turning back to Ivy. "Thanks. I'd like that." Carlee didn't know Ivy well. She'd only recently joined the MC club and become Steele's Little girl when Carlee had entered into the fateful relationship with Silver. She knew Ivy was very kind and fun though.

Ivy beamed. "Do you like toaster waffles? Daddy said I could have the blueberry ones this morning as long as I also eat an egg and drink something healthy."

"I love toaster waffles," Carlee responded before suddenly twisting around to glance at Atlas. This was all so new to her, but she wanted to be a well-behaved Little girl who made him proud.

He smiled. "That's a great idea, Baby girl. Thank you for checking with me."

She beamed, standing taller and holding her head higher at his praise. She might have even skipped alongside Ivy.

When they reached the kitchen, a few other club members were standing around the coffeepot. Doc, Gabriel, and Talon. They all looked up and smiled. No one seemed shocked.

Gabriel waved. "Hey, Carlee. Nice to see you."

Talon tipped his head. "Ditto, Little one. That dress looks so pretty on you."

Doc nodded. "It's been a while. I'm glad you're back. Atlas said you had a concussion a while back. I'd like to take a look at you when you have time."

"Thank you," she managed to say in response to everyone before looking at Doc. "I'm fine. I don't need a doctor."

Atlas set his hand on her neck and squeezed. "Not optional, Baby girl. We'll go see Doc at some point today."

She sighed. She knew she wasn't going to get out of that.

Doc, Talon, and Gabriel turned back to their conversation, sipping coffee.

Atlas pulled out a chair at the table and helped Carlee into it.

Steele did the same for Ivy next to her.

Carlee was mesmerized watching this scene unfold. Even though she'd hung around the club most of her life, she'd never been on this side of the fence. She'd never been someone's Little girl. She'd been Remi's friend, but nothing else.

She wasn't unaware of the intimate interactions between Daddies and Littles in the club, but to her they'd always just seemed normalized. She hadn't paid close attention.

Now she was someone's Little. She was sitting at the table watching two men cook for their girls. Surreal didn't begin to describe things.

Ivy caught her attention. "Daddy says he's going to help Atlas in the office this morning. He said I could hang out with you. Maybe we can color or do puzzles."

Carlee had never felt more like she belonged before in her life. Like she was home. It wasn't a physical thing. She'd been here in the compound thousands of times. But this was different. Now she was sort of a member. Not just of the MC itself but of the Littles' club.

"That sounds like fun." She let her feet swing under her chair, feeling lighter when she thought this morning would be scary and stressful. Ivy was making it perfect.

Ivy grinned. "I'm so glad. Maybe Remi can join us if she comes today."

Carlee nodded as Atlas set two sippy cups in front of her. One with juice. One with milk. Just like yesterday. Because he was thoughtful and remembered things.

A few minutes later, he brought a plate over at the same time as Steele. It was filled with scrambled eggs, bacon, and toaster waffles. "Tell me when," he said as he lifted a bottle of syrup.

She stopped him, tipping the syrup back upright in his hand just in time before it dripped out of the bottle.

"You don't like syrup, Baby girl?"

She looked at him, feeling silly. "I do, but can I have it on the side in a small bowl, please, Daddy?" Would he think she was too silly? Would he refuse her, not wanting to waste another dish?

Instead, he smiled. "Ah, you don't want to get syrup on your eggs, do you?"

She shook her head.

He turned around, grabbed a bowl from the cabinet, and set it in front of her before pouring the syrup. "Let me know if you want more, Baby girl." He set the bottle down out of reach at the huge table. He wasn't going to let her pour it. That made her feel all tingly and special inside.

"Thank you, Daddy." She knew she was nearly beaming with happiness. He kept surprising her. He kept getting better and better. He was too good to be true.

If she'd poured syrup in a separate bowl while she'd been living with Silver, he would have told her she was ungrateful and wasteful. He wasn't here though. He would never hurt her again. Not emotionally or physically.

Carlee and Ivy ate their breakfast while giggling about the tiny fake blueberries in the waffles and the way the bacon crunched and fell apart on their plates.

The men sat across from them with plates piled high with eggs and bacon. They were even having toaster waffles too. Apparently Littles weren't the only ones who enjoyed frozen waffles.

When they were done, Atlas removed her plate and wiped

her sticky fingers on a wet cloth before lifting her to set her on her feet.

Doc, Talon, and Gabriel had left the kitchen, but as they were finishing, Remi came barreling in. She was all smiles and nearly knocked Carlee on her ass as she slammed into her with a huge hug. "Daddy says we get to have a playday," she shouted, glancing at Ivy.

Ivy grinned and nodded too before turning toward Steele. "Can we go now?"

Steele frowned. "Go where? You need to stay where we can see you."

Ivy groaned. "Can't we go outside? It's nice out."

"No." It was Atlas who put his foot down even harder, shaking his head, frowning. "I want Carlee inside. I want you girls to stay in the community room where someone can keep an eye on you."

Ivy turned toward Steele. "Daddy..." she groaned.

Steele lifted a brow so high Carlee thought it might pop off the top of his forehead.

He didn't even have to say a word for Ivy to back down and cower. "Sorry, Daddy. We'll stay in the community room."

Atlas took Carlee's chin in his hand and leaned down so his face was close to hers. "I suspect your bottom is still red hot from this morning. Would you like me to add to it?"

She clenched her thighs together. This was the first time he was reprimanding her in public. The first time anyone had ever done so. She needed a few seconds to process how she felt about his words and who was witnessing her discipline.

While she stared at him, he waited. He was processing too. Watching her, she realized. Waiting to see her reaction. She knew the backs of her thighs were bright red and anyone who looked would already see that because her dress was barely long enough to cover her panties.

Carlee could feel all four sets of eyes on her. They could see her thighs because her back was to them. They could see her short pink dress, frilly socks, pigtails, ribbons. They could also see the way she trembled.

What they could not see was the wetness that leaked out to soak her panties or the way her nipples puckered hard against the front of her dress.

Atlas could though. He glanced down briefly at her nipples and back, giving nothing away in his expression. Finally, he cupped the back of her head and leaned down farther and to the side to set his lips on her ear.

He whispered softly so no one could hear him, "Are your panties wet, Baby girl?"

She swallowed and nodded.

"Good girl. Do you want to continue this argument here in front of everyone or go play?"

"Go play, Sir," she whispered. There were flutters from a million butterflies in her tummy though. She wasn't sure she wanted her Daddy to spank her in front of people, but she was aware the threat of him doing so was titillating. So much so that she was wobbly.

He rose to his full height. "Stay in the main room. I don't even want you to go potty without someone with you. Understood?"

"Yes, Sir." She turned and joined Ivy and Remi who had moved closer to the door. The butterflies didn't stop though, and when she looked over her shoulder, she found Atlas smiling knowingly.

She didn't breathe easier until the three of them were out of sight, and even then she was still sort of panting. And she missed him. She didn't like him being out of her sight. If he kept her panting like this, she was going to need to start carrying that inhaler around with her.

Remi took her hand as they walked. "I wonder when it's going to stop being weird seeing you with my brother."

Carlee shrugged. "Girl, I wonder when it's going to stop being weird seeing me with your brother too."

Ivy giggled. "Do you think he'll stay in town? Steele said he's only here for a month."

"I'm not sure yet. Every time the subject comes up, he deflects. He says we'll talk about it later."

"What if he decides to go back home to his job?" Remi asked.

They had reached the community room, and Carlee stopped walking and looked at her friends. She wiped her palms on the front of her dress. "He's my Daddy." Her lip was trembling. There was no way she would stay behind if he wanted to go back to the city. She would die.

Remi pulled her in for a hug. "It will be okay. I promise." They rocked and hugged. Ivy joined the group hug.

After a few minutes, they stood back and Ivy announced, "Let's play cards." She rushed across the room to the game closet and pulled it open.

Carlee took a deep breath. This was the first official day of her new life. She wanted to embrace it to its fullest.

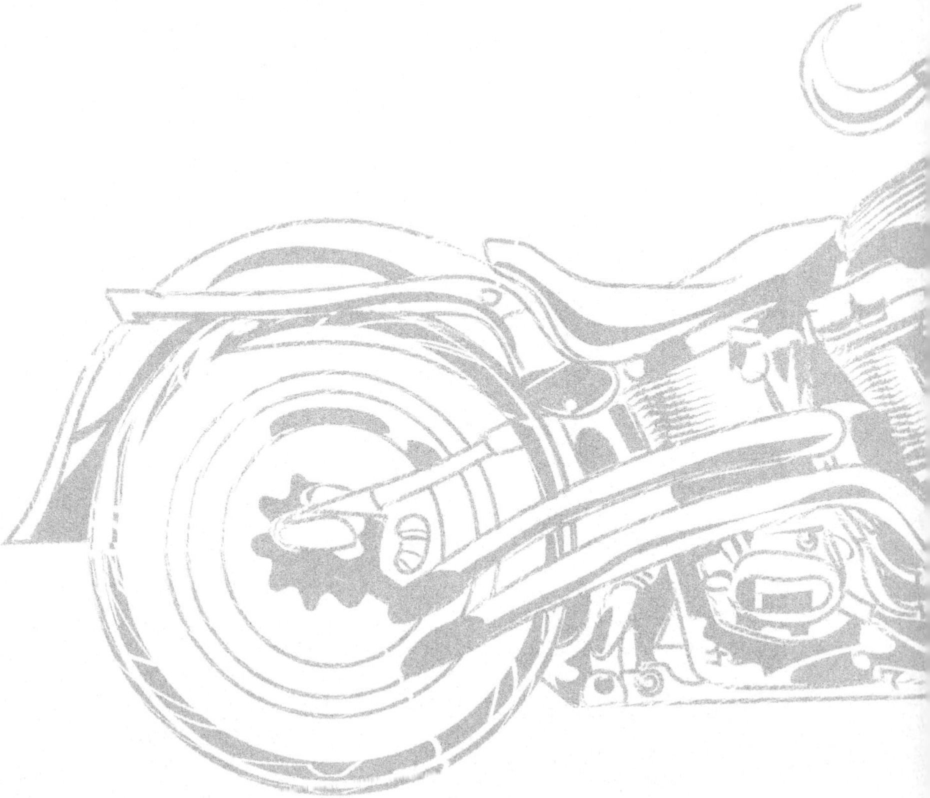

CHAPTER
THIRTEEN

"You're worried," Gabriel stated unnecessarily later that afternoon.

Atlas leaned back in his chair and reached his hands behind his head to clasp his fingers at the back of his neck. "Yes."

As many club members as were around and available this afternoon had gathered in the conference room directly off the community room. Atlas wanted to bring everyone up to speed, but he wanted to be able to keep his eyes on Carlee through the open door at all times.

"I assume you found things we'd all rather not know were happening under our noses with the treasurer," Doc said.

Atlas nodded and drew in a breath. "Silver was lying to everyone for years. The books are a disaster. Not just recently but for a long time. He's been siphoning the club's money too."

"Fuck," Talon grunted. "How much?"

"Hard to say since he kept horrible books and didn't document many things, but the bank account I can see. It took a few hard hits before he disappeared. Based on the calendar on the wall in the office, I'd say he was stealing money on weekends."

Bear rubbed his beard where he stood against the wall, unwilling to sit at the table. "He was gambling. Bragged about it often enough. Drove out of town on weekends to hit casinos. I bet he was fucking losing his ass."

"That's my suspicion," Atlas confirmed.

"Do you suppose he owed someone money, and that's why he took off?" Steele asked.

"Maybe. Or he just knew his days were numbered before he was found out."

"Meanwhile he was treating Carlee like shit." Kade scowled.

"Yes." Atlas nodded. He hated this for her, but everyone needed to know who hadn't heard. "He was no Daddy. He was an abuser. He took over her life, sold her trailer, made her quit her job, and isolated her from her friends. She lived as a domestic slave for three months until he backhanded her so hard she slammed into the wall and got a concussion."

"Fuck," Storm shouted. "We should have known."

Atlas shook his head. "You couldn't have known. Even Remi didn't know."

Faust ran a hand over his head. "Silver was good. He made it seem like she was so into him that she didn't want to come to the club anymore. And when she left him, he told everyone all she did was nag him about getting out of the MC. That she hated the MC and wanted him to live an honest life—as if we aren't honest men. I can't for the life of me imagine why the fuck we even entertained any of Silver's nonsense. We've known Carlee since she was a child. We should have been suspicious."

Gabriel turned toward Atlas. "I'd like to apologize. I know you weren't here, but Carlee is your girl now, and the club let her down. I feel personally responsible for not checking up on her and making sure she was okay."

"We all do," Steele agreed.

Atlas nodded. "Thank you. I know Carlee will appreciate hearing that. She's got a strong, fierce heart. She doesn't blame anyone except Silver. He was with the club for a very long time. He threatened her life if she came around or badmouthed him. She took that threat seriously and made herself scarce out of self-preservation."

Steele set his palms on the table and leaned in. "She *is* your Little girl now, right?"

"Absolutely." Atlas had no doubt about that. He glanced again into the main room where she was sitting on the floor with Ivy and Remi putting a puzzle together.

He breathed easier every time he checked on her.

"She needs protection at all times," Kade stated.

"Every moment," Atlas agreed, relieved everyone was taking this seriously.

"If Silver comes snooping around or returns to the club, who knows what he might do if he finds her here," Gabriel pointed out.

Atlas rubbed a hand down his face. "Well, she's not leaving the compound without me. She knows to stay where one of us can see her at all times. We can't lock her up any tighter than that. As it is she's going to get antsy eventually. It could be months or years or never before Silver shows up."

Steele nodded slowly. "You're right. I'll put out some feelers to the other MCs in the nearby towns and see if anyone has seen him and let them know of the situation so if he shows up anywhere, someone will inform us."

"Thank you," Atlas said.

"Let's adjourn for now," Steele suggested as he rose to his feet. "I'm sure everyone is feeling a bit unnerved."

As the members filed out of the room, Atlas stepped out too. He glanced around for his father and headed in his direction. The man was standing at the door as if he were personal security assigned to the girls. Atlas had already spoken to him and filled him in on everything, so Rock hadn't needed a rehash at the meeting. Plus, he felt more useful keeping watch.

"Everything go okay?" Rock asked when Atlas joined him.

Atlas made eye contact with Carlee and gave her a reassuring smile. "Yes. Everyone understands. As I knew they would. No one believes Silver over Carlee. Plus, he's missing and he stole money, so there was no real contest."

"Didn't figure. I know your Little girl is stressed though. It's understandable. Now what?"

"Now we wait."

"For how long?"

"As long as it takes."

Rock turned to face outside. "You going to take Carlee and leave town?"

"Not immediately, no."

Rock nodded slowly. "But eventually..."

"I'm not sure anymore, Dad," he responded honestly. "I think it would be too hard on Carlee. She belongs here. These are her people. If I took her away, she would lose her support group. Remi and the other Littles who are her friends. People she needs. She's surrounded by love here."

"What about you, son? Do you love her?"

"With every ounce of my soul, Dad. Picked out a ring this morning," he announced quietly.

Rock gasped and glanced at him. A slow smile spread wide on his face. "No shit."

"No shit." Atlas couldn't keep from grinning also.

"I guess when you know, you know. That's how it was with your mom. She was my life."

Atlas set a hand on his dad's shoulder. "I know she was. Times like this I miss her terribly even though she's been gone over half my life."

"She would be so proud of you kids. Both of you." Rock glanced back again, and Atlas knew he was looking at Remi.

"She is, Dad. I'm sure she's watching from above."

Rock met his gaze. "You're going to get married."

"As soon as possible."

Rock chuckled. "Of course. You always did put a plan into action the moment you developed it. I'm surprised you didn't drag her to the justice of the peace this morning. Hell, why did you even wait until today?" He laughed harder.

"I am a determined man. That's for sure."

"And she's on board with this?"

"I think she's been half in love with me since she was about fifteen. Maybe I could have been too if I'd been looking. But I was in college and busy, and no way would I have fucked up my life by glancing at a girl who wouldn't have been legal to glance at in all fifty states."

"Probably a good plan since you claimed her in about five minutes the other night."

Atlas smiled again. "I had no idea it would feel like this, but Jesus, my heart. It's hers. Everything of mine is hers."

"I hate to say this because it's the last thing in the world I want, and I'm sure Carlee would hate it too, but maybe she would be safer if you took her to the city. Do you think?"

Atlas drew in a long breath. "The thought has occurred to me, but then I look at her and know it would break a piece of her. I would have to go to the office. I work long hours. She wouldn't be able to leave my apartment. Not at all. It would fucking send me into a panic if she were left alone. She'd be bored and grow resentful within days. At least here in town, everyone will look out for her. She misses her books. She misses working at the library. I was thinking I should go talk to the head librarian and see if there was any way Carlee could get her old job back or at least volunteer."

"You are a kind, thoughtful, good man and an amazing Daddy. I'm so damn proud of you my chest hurts." He slapped Atlas on the back. "In the meantime, here's an idea, why doesn't Carlee work on organizing and expanding the library here in the compound. Everyone here loves being able to pick up a book without having to go to the public library. Not just the Littles, but the Daddies too. I bet people have books in their homes and in their rooms they've already read. They could donate them."

"It's a good idea. I'll talk to her about it." Atlas stared out the door, seeing nothing. "If I stay, I'll need to find a job."

"If you stay, I'm sure there will be a unanimous vote to make you the new treasurer."

Atlas pondered his dad's words. Maybe the man was right. Atlas would still want to find work outside of the MC. Managing the club's financial business would be a mess for a while, but once it got straightened out, it would not be a full-time job for Atlas. Maybe he could go into private practice. He'd been working for a large firm for so long he'd forgotten what it would feel like to work for himself. There was probably a need for more accountants in town. It wouldn't be anything like the larger accounts he'd been handling for ten years, but it could be equally rewarding.

If Atlas dug deep and fully examined his life, he would have to admit he was exhausted. He'd been working himself to the bone to climb the corporate ladder for years. He had nothing but money to show for it. What good was money if he didn't have a life partner or time for vacation?

He'd been sleeping in a lonely apartment, trudging to work and back, and partying with superficial work friends on weekends. He'd been going through the motions of living without fully living at all.

Now that he was seeing the world through a new lens, he knew his life was with Carlee. His life *was* Carlee. There was no way he would take her to the city and force her to fit a mold she would hate. He had a distaste for it too.

He'd done what he'd set out to do back in high school. He'd gotten out of this town, made something of himself, and climbed the corporate rungs. It was time to make a change.

Suddenly, Atlas knew what needed to be done with such

clarity that his father must have seen it on his face. Rock started chuckling. "Guess you made up your mind."

Atlas snorted. "Yes." A list formed in his head. He needed to give notice. He needed a ring. He needed to find a home nearby where his Little girl could be happy. Nothing else mattered. It was so simple. He didn't even know what he'd been fretting over.

"Good luck. I'm happy for you," Rock said. "And Carlee is a lucky Little girl."

"Not half as lucky as I am," Atlas mused. "I hit the jackpot when I pulled off the road the other night to rescue her from her deathtrap car."

Rock laughed again. "Better add new wheels to your list of things to do. Talk to some of the other Daddies. They know better than anyone lately which are the safest cars on the road for Little girls."

Atlas cringed at the thought of Carlee driving away from him in a car. He knew it was irrational though. He couldn't hover over her forever. She would suffocate. She was a competent citizen. She could drive and take care of herself. The problem was he didn't want her to have to anymore. Atlas wanted to take care of everything. He wanted to make up for all the years she'd been on her own. Most of her life she'd had to fend for herself.

Not anymore. Never again. Carlee Marie Deveraux would never know that kind of loneliness again.

When he turned toward Carlee, he found her watching him. She wasn't helping with the puzzle or talking to the other girls. She was staring at him with a smile on her face, and then she tipped her head to the side and grinned wider.

Her cheeks were pink, and Lord have mercy, she bit her bottom lip. The little imp was goading him. The moment she sat up taller and smoothed her hands down her dress, causing the tight pebbles of her nipples to stand out, the blood ran from his face.

"Gotta go," he murmured to his dad. He took long strides to get to her and swept her off the floor and into his arms without a word.

She giggled as he tossed her over his shoulder and carried her from the room. He needed to be inside her. He was insatiable with her. He needed to see her pink bottom, which would still be hot and tingly from early that morning.

"I didn't even get to say goodbye to my friends," she cried out as he hauled her into their room and kicked the door shut.

"They'll understand." He lowered her onto the bed, pulling her dress over her head at the same time.

She wasn't laughing any longer. In fact when he rolled her onto her tummy and pulled her panties down her legs, she switched to moaning.

He didn't bother removing her shoes and socks. He didn't even remove her panties. He left them around her knees as he cupped her fucking sexy ass with both hands before lowering his face.

He needed to taste her. He needed to remind himself she was his. He needed to remind *her* she was his. He suspected he was going to need this validation a lot in the coming days.

Hell, he was glad he had a good excuse to put his foot down and demand she never be out of his sight. It would keep him from pacing and fidgeting. He needed her.

"Daddy…" His name was a musical moan as she arched her bottom up higher, giving him better access to her pussy, which he took full advantage of, finding her tight channel with his tongue and burying it deep.

"Oh, God…" She fisted the sheets next to her head and stretched her little body.

Atlas kissed a line up her spine until he reached her neck. He unfastened his jeans and lowered the zipper with one hand while he whispered in her ear, "I need to be inside you, Baby girl."

She whimpered. "Please, Daddy."

He reached for the nightstand, snagged a condom, and managed to tug his jeans and underwear over his hips in record time. Rolling the condom on forced him to let go of her for ten seconds before he gripped her hips and lined his cock up with her entrance.

He thrust all the way home between her thighs. She could barely get them wide enough with her panties restricting her legs. He liked it. It was fucking hot.

And the way she gripped the covers, the way she lifted her head to arch her chest, the fucking delightful moan that came from her mouth. All these things made his dick so hard it was threatening to erupt too soon.

"Carlee," he cried out. He yanked her hips back, causing her ass to rise so he could get his hand under her and play with her clit.

She shuddered. "Oh, God. Gonna come."

"That's the idea," he promised.

Moments later, her channel tightened around his cock as her orgasm milked him hard enough to take him over the edge right alongside her.

Heaven. That was the only word Atlas kept repeating over and over in his head today. He wanted to stay here. Stay right in heaven. Forever.

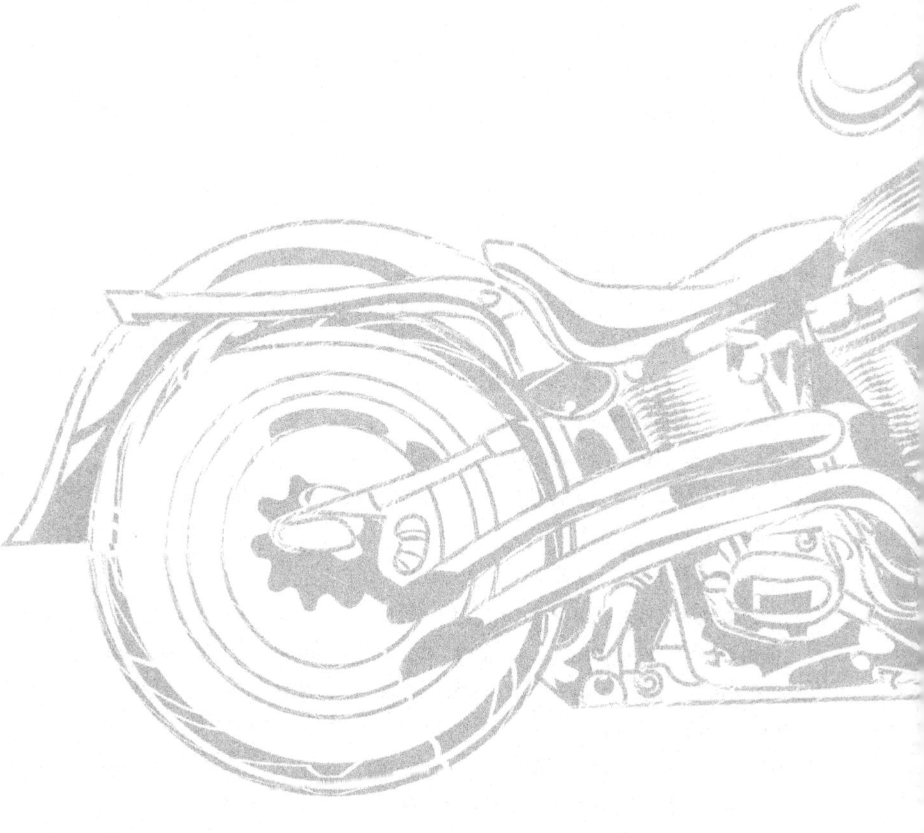

CHAPTER
FOURTEEN

"Daddy..." Carlee groaned a few hours later. "I'm telling you I'm fine. I don't need Doc to look at me. It's been like three months since I had that concussion."

Atlas ignored her protests as a knock sounded at the door. He opened it to let Doc in. He shook his hand before shutting the door.

Carlee was sitting on the edge of the bed. Her face felt hot. She hadn't seen a doctor in years. She didn't need one now either. Especially not a club member. What if he wanted to examine her intimately?

Daddy pulled the desk chair over so it was facing Carlee, and Doc took a seat.

He smiled warmly at her. "I heard you had a concussion a while back that was never confirmed."

She sighed. "Yeah."

"Carlee..." Daddy warned in a firm voice.

She sat up straighter. It would probably be best if she was polite and got this over with. "I knew I had all the symptoms, but I didn't have money to pay for medical care. I stayed in bed two days and worked through the headache and the nausea."

Doc's brows were furrowed. He set a hand on her forehead, pulled her eyelid up, and lifted a light to flash in her eye before doing the same on the other side. "And you haven't had any symptoms since then?"

"No, Sir. None. The headaches lingered for a few days, but then I felt fine."

"No more nausea?"

"No, Sir." She shook her head. Maybe he would keep it simple and be done.

He met her gaze. "It was dangerous for you to stay alone after a concussion. Please don't ever do something like that again. Okay, Little girl?"

"Yes, Sir. I promise."

"Now, Atlas tells me you also have asthma. How has that been going?"

Oh, great... "I hardly ever have any incidents anymore. I've mostly outgrown it."

"Except the other night," Daddy pointed out. "She got winded climbing the stairs to her apartment."

Ugh. "Yeah, but that was also because I was stressed when I found my super standing outside my door. It was a double whammy."

"I'd like to listen to your heart and lungs, Little one," Doc said. "Let's pull your dress off so I can listen closely."

Carlee's heart started beating rapidly as Daddy reached over and pulled her dress over her head. If they wanted her to have symptoms of asthma, they were going to get their wish.

"Sit up tall for me, Little one," Doc requested as he rubbed the flat metal disk of his stethoscope.

Carlee panted as she did as she was told. She was naked except for her panties now. Embarrassed. And the worst part was her nipples were hard. Maybe because it was cold in the room. But she knew that was a lie. It was because she was totally turned on by this humiliation. That realization embarrassed her further.

Doc stood, set a hand on her back, and held the stethoscope to her chest between her boobs. He moved it around, listening intently. "Take a deep breath for me."

She drew in a slow breath as deep as she could.

"Good girl. Let it out slowly."

He repeated this several times. His knuckles grazed her nipples several times too. He didn't comment. When he switched to listening to her back, he braced himself with his free hand on her chest.

"I filled her inhaler prescription the night I got here," Daddy told him.

Doc smiled when he finished. "Lungs sound good. Keep an eye on her while she's going through this stressful time, and keep the inhaler handy just in case."

Carlee hoped he was finally done.

"Can you lie back for me, Little one?"

Apparently not.

Daddy came to her other side and helped her recline on the bed.

"Lift your arms over your head for me, Carlee," Doc requested.

Carlee thought she might actually die all stretched out like this in front of Doc in nothing but her panties. Little girl panties. She prayed he wouldn't make her take them off.

He set his hands on her stomach. "Any tummy issues, Little one?"

"No, Sir," she murmured as he palpated her belly.

He glanced at her several times as he poked all around, up under her ribs and down to her pelvis.

She squeezed her legs together. *Please don't make me take my panties off. Please don't make me take my panties off.*

"When was the last time you saw a gynecologist, Little one?"

Oh, God. She swallowed. "It's been a long time."

Doc looked at Daddy. "I'd get her an appointment with a local ob/gyn. I'll give you a name. Regular well-woman checkups are important."

Daddy nodded. "I'll call them right away."

Doc smiled at her again. "Everything sounds good, Carlee. Your heart and lungs. Your tummy feels fine. Let me know if you have any trouble breathing. That's not something to mess with."

"Okay, Sir."

He pulled up the desk chair and sat next to where she lay on the bed. He set a hand on hers. His face was serious. "Have you had any testing for STDs since your previous relationship?"

Her face heated as she swallowed. "Yes, Sir," she whispered. "I went to a free clinic right away."

He smiled and patted her hand. "Good girl. And I'm so glad you're back in the MC. Everyone is going to keep a close eye on you and keep you safe."

"Thank you." She tried to control the shiver that took over her body. She was having a full discussion with Doc while her boobs were exposed. Could she please have her dress back?

But Daddy was holding the dress, and he didn't give it back to her. In fact, he tucked it under his arm as he walked Doc to the door and saw him out. When he turned around, he was smirking.

"Can I have my dress back?" Carlee asked in a small voice as she started to sit up.

"Mmm. I don't think so." Daddy grabbed her wrists and hauled them back over her head. He held them in one hand as he leaned over and kissed her between her breasts.

Her breath hitched.

"You're aroused," he pointed out.

Her cheeks heated. "That's cause you're kissing me."

He chuckled. "Fibber." He slid a hand down between her

thighs and cupped her pussy without warning. "You're soaked."

She bit her lip, not wanting to tell lies he would see right through.

"Your nipples were so hard while Doc listened to your heart. You liked the embarrassment." He wasn't asking. He was pointing out the obvious.

No sense trying to deny it.

"I should have had him take a look at your red bottom to make sure I'm not striking you too hard."

She was beyond glad he hadn't done that. It would have mortified her, and soaked her panties.

"Mmm," he mused. "Next time."

"Daddy..." she murmured. Would he please stop tormenting her?

He smiled. "There's nothing to be embarrassed about. Little girls often get aroused from a medical exam."

She pursed her lips. Couldn't he see she was embarrassed?

Yeah, he could see. He could see she liked it too. Her damn traitorous body had gotten totally aroused from the exposure and discussion about her body.

Daddy's face grew serious. "I am going to get you an appointment with a local gyno. Are you on any form of birth control?"

She shook her head. "No. I couldn't afford it."

"We can talk about that with the doctor and see what's best for us."

"You're going to go with me?" she asked incredulously.

"Of course. Your health is the most important thing in the world. I want to be a part of it." He winked at her and gave her a wicked grin. "Besides, I'm pretty sure whoever Doc recommends will be aware of the kink community."

Carlee groaned and squeezed her thighs together tighter. She would for sure be naked at a gyno visit. And there would be no way to hide her arousal from the doctor or her Daddy if he went into the room with her. She would end up needing that inhaler.

Daddy leaned over and kissed her so deeply she moaned into his mouth. Her body was on fire with need, even though they'd had sex not long ago. Her panties were soaked and her breasts felt heavy, her nipples hard points that demanded attention.

When Daddy broke the kiss, he whispered against her lips, "You were such a good girl for Doc, I think you deserve a reward." His hand slid between her legs again to stroke over her panties while he lowered his mouth to her nipple.

Carlee arched her chest clear off the bed. Thank God for rewards.

CHAPTER
FIFTEEN

T*wo weeks later...*

"Ten more minutes, Baby girl," Atlas called out from where he was standing at the back door to the club.

"Okay, Daddy," Carlee responded from the swings where she was pumping her legs so that she was going higher than he liked.

The sun would be going down soon. Atlas had loosened his tight grip on the reins and let her go outside for a while every day, but it still made him nervous.

He sighed as he turned back toward Gabriel. "So, you'll officiate the wedding for us?"

"Of course. I'd be honored. Name the date and time and I'm there. Does she know yet?"

"Not specifically. She has to suspect I'm carrying around a ring, waiting for the right moment to put it on her finger. Part of the fun is that she probably expected me to slide it on her starting about ten days ago. I'm making her fidget."

Gabriel chuckled. "You are devious."

"I call it delayed gratification," Atlas declared.

"She's been loosening up more and more every day. You're good for her," Gabriel stated. "I've known her for years, and I've never seen her this happy."

"I hope so." Another glance showed her pigtails flying. Her skirt was lifting every time she pumped too. She'd gotten less self-conscious about people seeing her panties.

Atlas had watched her closely and determined he would not expose her bottom in public spaces. At first he'd insisted it was because she was too embarrassed, but eventually he'd admitted to himself that he didn't want other people to see her pink little pussy or how wet she got when he reprimanded her.

He could live with her panties showing. They covered more of her than the bikinis most women wore. But he wouldn't share her pussy or her bare nipples.

"How are the accounting books coming along?" Gabriel asked.

Atlas knew the man was standing outside the back door with him mainly to keep him company while Carlee got fresh air and exercise and could play. Atlas appreciated the company. "I think I'm finally all caught up. It was a mess, but the MC books are in order now. Missing a lot of money Silver siphoned off mind you. A *lot*. Things are going to be tight for a while."

"Yeah. That's disturbing."

"From now on there needs to be two people keeping checks and balances on the books. I'm training one of the younger guys, Talon, who has shown an affinity for math. I know the club unanimously voted me in as treasurer, and I appreciate the vote of confidence, but no one should hold all the club's power like that. It's dangerous."

"Good point," Gabriel agreed, meeting Atlas's gaze and holding it with a serious expression. "I know everyone has told you this, but we're all beyond glad you're here and even more pleased you've decided to stay."

Atlas nodded at him. "Thank you. The decision was easy."

"Rock says you'll be starting your own practice in town."

"That's my plan. Far less stressful than working for a huge firm in the city." His boss had been disappointed to hear that Atlas wouldn't be returning, but the man said he hadn't really been all that surprised. Not once he found out Atlas had an extended family somewhere else who needed him.

"Did some of the prospects go clear out your apartment for you?" Gabriel asked.

"Yes. They did a fantastic job. I was so grateful not to have to leave Carlee to go myself. I settled up with the apartment manager to get out of my lease. It's a done deal now. I'm officially back with the Shadowridge Guardians," Atlas announced with pride.

Something caught Atlas's attention out of the corner of his eye near the gate, and he lifted his head to find a man staggering toward them. He had a gun in his hand, and he was waving it around haphazardly.

"Heard you thought you could swoop in here and take what was mine," the man slurred. He was drunk.

Atlas jerked his gaze toward the swings, and his heart fell from his chest. Carlee was nowhere in sight. The swing was still moving as if she'd jumped from it, but she was gone.

Atlas looked back to the man. Four other club members were behind him, inching along, following him, but not getting too close. Not surprising since the fucker had a gun in his hand.

"Silver…" Gabriel growled. "You're not welcome here anymore. What do you want?"

Atlas wasn't surprised to learn this was Silver. Though he'd seen him plenty of times in the past, he wouldn't have recognized him today. He had long greasy hair, deep, bloodshot eyes, and a hollow gaunt face. He'd lost weight, and he looked like death.

Silver cackled. "Want what's mine." He lifted the gun and aimed it at Atlas.

"Put the gun down, Silver," Gabriel called out.

Atlas stood very still. He would not cower in front of this motherfucker, but he didn't want to make any sudden movements that might get him shot either.

Where the fuck is Carlee?

Had Silver gotten to her first? That seemed unlikely. But Atlas wasn't ruling it out.

"What do you think is yours, Silver?" Atlas asked, his voice even and forceful.

Silver cackled again, swaying so hard to one side that he staggered a bit. "Don't play stupid with me, Mister High and Mighty. Think you can come to town, take my job and my girl?"

Fuck. So this *was* about Carlee. Atlas had suspected this day would come. That was why he'd put so many safeguards in place. It was why he only let Carlee play outside when he was with her. It was why even though he'd spoken to the head librarian at the public library and secured her a job, he still hadn't let her start. It was why even though he'd looked at cars for her, he still hadn't purchased one. It was why he was in a complete and total panic right now.

"You left, Silver," Atlas stated in a voice far calmer than he felt. "Did you think no one was going to take over your position within the club? It's been a month." Atlas could sense people coming up behind him.

"Put the gun down, Silver," Kade said, his voice loud as he stepped between Atlas and Gabriel. "You don't want anyone to get hurt. If you start shooting that thing, we'll shoot back. If you put it down, we can talk about what you want man to man."

Silver leaned his head back and laughed toward the sky. "What I want?"

"Yes." This voice was Steele's. "Let's go somewhere and talk."

Silver lifted the gun and swung it around in a half circle, aiming at everyone and no one. "Ain't nothin' to talk about. Where is my girl? She might not be much to look at, but she cleans a mean house and can cook better'n my mom. Plus her cunt is nice and tight. She fights me when I fuck her too. Gets my juices running, ya know? I love a woman who puts up a fight."

Atlas's blood was boiling. He wanted to charge forward and strangle this piece of shit, but the man wasn't worth it. Not worth getting arrested over. That was for sure. And Atlas could hear sirens in the distance. Had someone called the cops?

It was possible. The Shadowridge Guardians were known for working with the police from time to time to apprehend someone.

Atlas considered approaching this man who mostly had a beef with him, but if Carlee was watching from somewhere nearby, she would panic and possibly freak out and inadvertently give away her location. Right now, Atlas wasn't yet sure if Silver had even seen her or not.

Silver tipped his head back again and started screaming. "Caarrrrlleee!"

Fuck. Please stay wherever you are, Baby girl.

Silver lifted his gun again and aimed it at Atlas. There was very little chance he could hit the broad side of a barn considering how drunk or high he was, but he might accidentally kill someone.

"Carlee, I know you're around here somewhere. This fucker who thinks he has some kind of claim on you wouldn't let you far out of his sight. Get your ass out here and come with me unless you want me to shoot this pretty boy from the city." It was actually shocking how clear Silver's speech was. He kept wavering in and out of levels of coherency. Surely drugs were involved.

"Stay right where you are, Carlee," Atlas shouted. "Do not move an inch." He prayed she would listen to him.

Silver stumbled a few feet closer, holding the gun up with both hands even though he kept swaying back and forth.

Not one man alongside Atlas or behind him—and several had accumulated—backed down. They presented a unified front.

"You shut the fuck up, asshole," Silver growled. "She ain't your girl. She's mine. Has she made you her fucking fried chicken?" He laughed wildly. "Shit's good. And her mashed po-ta-toes too. Cain't make gravy worth a shit, but she was a'learnin'. *Carlee*," he screamed again. "What did I tell you, bitch? I believe I told you not to come back to this MC. I'll whip your ass for disobeying me."

Atlas's jaw tightened. He hated this man with every molecule of his being. Hated the way he was antagonizing Carlee who undoubtedly could hear him just fine from wherever she was hiding.

By now, Atlas was at least convinced Silver didn't have her. He wouldn't have been standing there bellowing if he already had her.

The sirens got closer.

Atlas wasn't sure if the approach of officers was about to be a help or a hindrance. And then he got his break.

Silver seemed to suddenly realize what all the noise was coming from the street. He twisted his head around to look toward the entrance. That was his mistake.

It took Atlas point five seconds to whip his weapon from where it was nestled in the back of his pants, aim, and fire.

Silver screamed, this time in pain, as he dropped his gun on the ground and grabbed his arm with his other hand. "Motherfucker!"

A dozen club members rushed forward, surrounding Silver, guns drawn. The first one to get close enough kicked the gun as far as he could. "On your knees, asshole." It was Bear. The guy was fierce when he needed to be.

Four cops rushed through the back gate, guns drawn. It didn't take long for them to realize what was going on and approach the moaning pile of shit on the ground.

Atlas was pretty sure he'd heard his Baby girl scream bloody murder when the gunshot went off, but he hadn't seen her yet. Carlee was his top priority now that plenty of people had Silver surrounded. Hell, cuffs were already going on him.

A paramedic would be along shortly, but Atlas was fine with them taking their sweet time checking out his good aim.

Atlas turned toward the side of the compound, pushing past everyone who had gathered. He needed Carlee in his arms. He needed to get her out of here. Where the hell was she?

He gave a silent thank you to God, his father, and every other man in the MC who'd spent countless hours supervising his target practice when he was younger. He hadn't held or shot a gun in many years until this past week, but he obviously hadn't lost his touch.

"Carlee," he called out as gently as possible over the din of commotion as he rounded the side of the building. He couldn't see her anywhere. Where was she?

"Atlas."

Atlas spun around at the sound of his name.

Remi was jogging toward him.

"What are you doing out here? You should be inside."

Kade was keeping stride behind her, brows furrowed.

"I know where she is," Remi panted.

"Where?"

She pointed toward the old oak tree next to the swings, her finger rising up into the branches.

Atlas smiled as he approached and slowly rounded the

enormous trunk, squinting up into the tree branches. Part of him wanted to paddle his Little girl's bottom hard for doing something so dangerous, but the larger part of him wanted to hug her fiercely and praise her for thinking so fast.

"Carlee?" He still couldn't see her. The leaves were thick and the branches were dense. He glanced at Remi who was also circling and looking, Kade right behind her. "How do you know?"

"Because that's where we always hid when we were kids."

"Hid from what?" Kade asked.

Atlas chuckled. "Hid from Dad when it was time to come inside." He remembered that, but he hadn't known where those two naughty girls had hidden. No one ever had as far as he knew.

"Carlee," he cooed again. "Baby, tell Daddy where you are so I can help you get down."

A whimper caught his attention, and he finally found her, curled up in a ball on a pretty high branch, leaning against the trunk.

"Hey, Baby girl," he said softly as he met her gaze. "It's safe now. You can come down."

She shook her head, which made him panic a bit for fear she would lose her balance and fall. "Don't wanna," she murmured.

"He's gone, Little one. The police are taking him away now."

She pulled her knees in tighter against her chest. Her panties were pale yellow and visible.

Atlas's heart thumped hard. He wanted her safely in his arms. He wanted to hold her tight and never let her go. But he needed to be cautious so he didn't upset her further or spook her.

"Do you want Daddy to come up there, Baby girl?" He glanced down at himself. "I'm kind of big, but I bet I could do it if I tried. Is there room for me?"

She finally giggled. "No, Daddy. You're too big."

"But what if I want to hold you? I can't do that with you up there and me down here. My arms are very sad without you in them."

"Scared," she whispered.

"I know you are, but it's over now, and Daddy is never going to let anything happen to you."

"Am I in trouble?" she asked in a very Little voice.

"No, Baby girl. Not at all. I'm so proud of you for running and hiding so fast. This was the safest place you could have gone. Silver never would have found you there. I can hardly see you through the branches and leaves, and I know where I'm looking. I'm so, so proud of you," he repeated. "But I really want to hug you now."

"You're sure it's safe?"

"Yes, Baby girl. I'm positive." He glanced toward the open gate of the compound. Silver and the police were both outside the gate now. An ambulance had pulled up.

Atlas knew someone would need to question him about the shot, but he would deal with that later. Steele would make sure no one bothered Atlas while he was trying to lure Carlee out of the tree.

"Okay, Daddy," she finally said.

He held his breath as she unfolded herself. There was no need though. His Little girl deftly climbed down as if she'd done this every day of her life. She was a little monkey. How had he never known that?

When she reached the lowest branch, she squatted down and held out her arms. "Catch me, Daddy." And then she jumped, barely giving him enough warning.

He caught her though, and he held on to her with his arms wrapped around her small body so tightly she probably couldn't breathe. He kissed all over her face. He was half aware that her dress was hiked up around her waist and her panties were showing to anyone around, but he couldn't bear to let her go to straighten her clothes.

She eventually started giggling. "Daddy, that tickles." She tipped her head back and from side to side to avoid his kisses all over her neck and behind her ears.

He finally stopped, but as soon as he let her slide to the ground, he cupped her face and held her gaze. "I love you more than life itself, Carlee Marie."

"I love you too, Daddy." Her face grew serious. "You shot him."

"I did." He nodded, his expression serious.

"Will he die?"

"No, Baby girl. I shot him in the arm so he would drop the gun. The police have him now."

Kade was still standing close. He cleared his throat. "Apparently no one from the club called the cops. Silver was wanted for several robberies in town. Someone spotted him heading toward our compound and called the police."

Atlas let out a relieved breath. It would be far tidier if Silver were convicted on a bunch of crimes that didn't involve the MC. It would keep several men from having to spend a great deal of time testifying about Silver's behavior within the club. It would also be preferable if Silver went down for enough other crimes that Carlee wouldn't need to make a court appearance either.

"It sounds like he's wanted for a laundry list of offenses." Kade slapped Atlas on the back before he wandered away.

"That's good, right?" Carlee asked.

"Yes, Baby girl. That's very helpful." He kissed her again, this time on the lips, deepening it, blocking out everyone around him. Fuck 'em. He was busy right now.

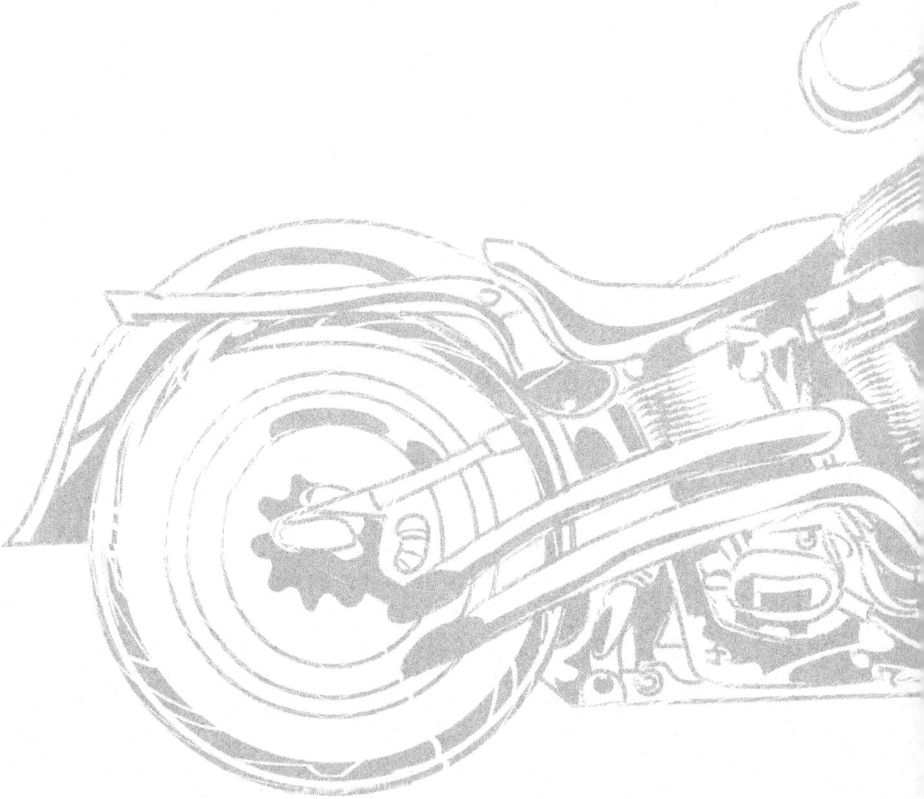

CHAPTER
SIXTEEN

It was hard for Atlas to keep a straight face the next morning when he awoke to find his Baby girl sitting next to him wide awake. She wasn't just sitting. She was cross-legged with her arms folded over her chest, her eyes narrowed, and the cutest pout on her lips.

Her hair was wild all around her head, and she was wearing a pale pink camisole. He never let her wear anything in their bed, so he was surprised to see she'd somehow managed to slip out of his arms, find the sexy camisole, and return to get into this obviously intentional position.

Atlas fought back the grin that wanted to spread as he rolled to his side, leaned his head on his palm, and looked up at her beautiful face. He didn't try to cover his morning hard-on, nor did he touch her. He simply looked at her.

He couldn't wait to hear what this pouty look was all about. "What's going on, sassy pants?" He knew the silly nickname would get under her skin.

She snorted. "Daddy…" The whine went with the nickname. She even hmphed, lifting and lowering her arms still crossed over her chest. She narrowed her gaze at him. "How long are you going to make me wait, meanie?"

He chuckled. He couldn't help himself. "Wait for what, sassy pants?" He reached out with one hand and lowered the thin strap of her camisole so it fell down her arm. He knew exactly what she wanted, but tormenting her was too much fun.

"*Daddy,*" she cried.

He lowered the other strap next. If she ever moved her folded arms, the sexy lingerie would fall down to her waist. "Who said you could get out of bed, snoop around in the drawers, and put on clothes?" he teased.

She leaned forward. "I would have put on more than just this camisole if I could have found it."

"Found what, sassy pants?" God, he loved teasing her.

She hmphed again. "You know what." She pushed her bottom lip out farther and pouted heavily. "How long are you going to make me wait? You almost died yesterday. What if you had died?" Her voice rose with each sentence.

He didn't want to make light of her frustration, but… "Daddy was never in danger of dying, Baby girl."

"He had a gun," she shouted. "He wanted to kill you."

Atlas ran his hand up the outside of her thigh and squeezed her ass. "He was drunk and high, Little one. He couldn't have shot anyone if he'd tried." He was exaggerating, but he didn't want her to be afraid. "I was watching him closely the entire time, waiting for an opportunity to disarm him."

She narrowed her eyes. "Still. I was scared and you—" Her breath hitched, and she pursed her lips, probably to keep from crying.

Atlas leaned over her so his chest was in her lap and he could reach around and tuck his hand under the mattress. A moment later, he righted himself. "Is this what you're waiting for, Baby girl?" He held up the diamond ring he'd been carrying around for two weeks.

She gasped and glanced over her shoulder. "Where did you

get that from?"

He chuckled. "Between the mattress and the box springs. Have you been looking for it all over the room when I'm not watching, naughty girl?"

She shrugged. "Maybe."

"What were you going to do if you found it?" he teased.

She sat taller and lifted her chin. "Put it on and wait for you to notice that we're engaged."

He laughed harder. "I don't think that's how it works. You told me you wanted me to ask you."

"But that was like ages ago. You never asked me. I've been waiting for like *ever*."

He grabbed her hip again. "You've been mine for two weeks. That's hardly forever."

"If you tell a girl you're going to marry her and that you're going to surprise her one day with a ring, all the days after that are like years, Atlas. Everyone knows that."

"Do they, now?" He tugged on her folded arms. "Do you want this ring? If you do, you're going to have to give me your left hand."

When she released her arms, her camisole fell to her waist. She glared at him. "You tricked me."

"Yes. Yes, I did. It was worth it too. I'm going to spank your cute bottom until you beg me to stop for snooping around and putting on clothes too. But first, I'll put you out of your misery."

"This isn't really *clothes*," she argued.

He held up the ring. "You want to argue semantics with Daddy, or do you want me to ask you to marry me?"

She drew in a deep breath and let her face relax. "I want you to ask me, Daddy."

Atlas rose up, slid off the side of the bed, and lifted her to her feet next to him. Her camisole fell to the floor, leaving her gloriously naked. Just the way he liked her.

He got down on one knee, took her hand, and tipped his

head back to meet her gaze. Not far. They were almost eye to eye with him on his knee. "Carlee Marie Deveraux, will you do me the honor of being my wife? Will you marry me and make me the happiest man and Daddy in the world?"

She smiled broadly. "Yes, Daddy. I'd love to marry you."

He slid the ring onto her finger and then kissed her knuckles.

She held it up and gasped. "The stone is so big. Daddy, it's huge."

"I wanted everyone around to know with a glance that my Baby girl is taken." He dropped his other knee so he was on both and pulled her sexy body flush against his, his hands on her hips. "I love you more than life itself, Carlee. I'm looking forward to a lifetime of your sassy silliness to keep me on my toes."

She cupped his face and kissed him. "I love you too, Daddy. And I promise to be your sassy pants often enough to keep my bottom warm and tingly most of the time."

He chuckled. "Shall we start now?"

She held her ring out to look at it. "Maybe I could enjoy a moment with my ring first."

"Or…" He lifted her up and tossed her onto the bed, face down. "Maybe you can enjoy staring at your ring from timeout in the corner after Daddy spanks your naughty bottom."

She squirmed to get away from him, but she was giggling.

When he pinned her to the bed, he leaned over and kissed her neck. "God, you're gorgeous. I'm so fucking lucky."

"You're gorgeous too, Daddy. I'm the luckiest. Will you make love to me just this once after you spank me?"

"I think we can make that exception just this once." He figured he would end up making that exception far more often than just this one time. But he didn't care. They were going to have a lifetime of sex and spankings. It was going to be the best life. He knew it in his bones.

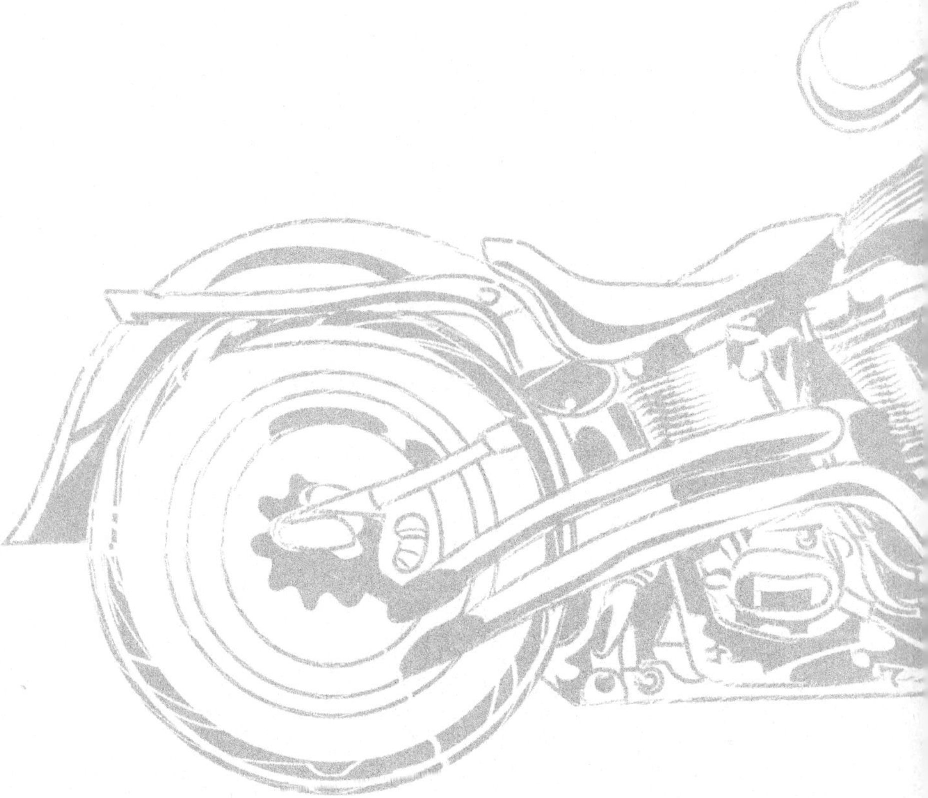

CHAPTER SEVENTEEN

A *week later...*

"Do you have a minute?"

Atlas glanced up from his desk to find Bear standing in the doorway to his new office space in town. He wasn't open for business yet, but he'd been working every day this week to get his new office ready.

"Hey. Come on in."

Bear looked over his shoulder before he grabbed a chair across from Atlas and took a seat.

Whatever brought Bear to Atlas's office in town instead of visiting him in the compound must have been important, especially if he was looking over his shoulder. "What's up?"

Bear leaned on one hip and pulled something out of his pocket. An envelope. He reached across the nearly empty desk and set it in front of Atlas, his hand still flattened on it. "I want you to have this for the club, but there's a catch."

Atlas frowned in confusion.

"You can't tell a soul. Ever."

Atlas licked his lips. "Okaayyy…" He couldn't imagine what Bear was talking about.

"I trust you. You're a good man." Bear held his gaze. "I have a reputation in the club, and it's important to me. I don't want anyone besides you to ever know where this came from."

Atlas searched his face, more confused than ever. "You have my word." Whatever was in the envelope, he hoped it wasn't illegal. He couldn't imagine Bear being involved in something illegal though.

Finally, Bear lifted his hand.

Atlas picked up the envelope and carefully opened it. What he pulled out was a check. He gasped. "Bear?"

Bear nodded. "The club needs it. I don't."

"But… Bear, that's a lot of zeros."

Bear shrugged. "Money means nothing to me. Is that enough to fix Silver's problems and get the club back in the black?"

Atlas's brows shot up. "Yes. More than enough. But…"

Bear shook his head and stood. "No buts. Just take it, and please don't tell anyone. Let it be anonymous. I promise it's clean." He chuckled. "I had a large inheritance. I just choose not to use it or tell anyone. I hate money."

Atlas stood also. "That's very generous of you. I don't know what to say. I will never tell a soul."

"Thank you." Bear tipped his head, turned, and left.

Atlas stood and watched Bear climb on his bike and drive away. He glanced down at the check again, too stunned for words. This was definitely going to fix the club's financial problems.

Atlas turned off his computer, packed up his bag, and headed for the door. He'd left Carlee at the public library. It was her first day back at work now that Silver had been apprehended and was no longer a threat.

Dropping her off this morning had made the Daddy side of

Atlas nervous, but he couldn't force her to stay in the clubhouse twenty-four/seven forever, especially now that he would be working in town part time himself. He was hoping to sync their schedules so he could drive her and pick her up when she worked.

He knew he was being overprotective. She needed her own car. He'd been looking. He would take her to pick one out soon, but he really preferred driving her himself, so he was procrastinating.

Atlas tucked his satchel in his saddlebag, climbed on his bike, and headed the few blocks to the library. It wasn't a coincidence he'd chosen a spot near his Little girl's place of employment.

After parking, he nearly jogged into the library. He hadn't been away from Carlee for this many hours since he'd picked her up from the side of the road.

Atlas entered the library with a grin on his face and scanned around, looking for Carlee. When he caught the eye of the head librarian behind the desk, she smiled and pointed toward a corner.

His heart raced as he headed in that direction. When he spotted Carlee sitting with another woman on a pair of beanbag chairs, he stopped moving, wanting to just watch her for a moment.

She was so carefree and happy, such a huge improvement over three weeks ago. She and the other woman were leaning over a book, giggling. Atlas suspected the other woman was Little also based on her mannerisms and the cute dress she was wearing. She had brown pigtails too. Just like Carlee.

Finally, Carlee lifted her head. She immediately beamed and jumped to her feet.

Atlas closed the distance between them and caught her out of the air when she threw herself into his arms. As soon as he could get to her mouth, he kissed her. "Missed you today, sassy pants," he teased in a soft voice.

"I missed you too, Daddy," she whispered. She turned around to the other woman. "This is my friend Brooke."

Atlas held out a hand as Brooke pushed to her feet. "Nice to meet you."

Brooke was flushed and took his hand shyly without looking directly at him.

"She loves books too," Carlee declared. "Maybe she could come over for a playdate sometime?"

"Of course, Little one." Brooke was definitely Little based on the way Carlee spoke of her. "Ready to go home, Baby girl?"

"Yep. I clocked out a while ago."

"Nice to meet you, Brooke." Atlas gave her a wave.

"You too," Brooke murmured. "See you later, Carlee."

By the time Atlas got Carlee out the door and over to his bike, she had told him a million things about her day, talking a mile a minute. He knew he'd made the right decision when he'd agreed she should go back to her library job. Anything that made his Little girl smile like this.

Before mounting the bike, Atlas took her in his arms and kissed her deeply. "I love you so much, Baby girl."

"I love you too, Daddy. How was your day? Did anything special happen?"

It sure had, but Atlas wouldn't be mentioning his meeting with Bear to anyone, not even Carlee. He'd made a promise, and he would keep it.

AUTHOR'S NOTE

I hope you're enjoying the Shadowridge Guardians MC series as much as we are enjoying writing them! The next book in the series is *Doc*, by Kate Oliver.

Doc by Kate Oliver

"Kitten, you're riding a fine line and once you cross it, you're going to be very sorry..."

Harper has just gotten her life back. After barely escaping her abusive ex-boyfriend, she's finally found a place she thinks she can call home. Shadowridge feels safe, and safe is what she needs more than anything right now.

Doc's convinced he'll never find the one for him. After all, no one wants to deal with a man who is as scarred and damaged as he is. No Little wants to deal with waking up to her Daddy having nightmares on the regular. But when he helps the timid Little girl with the scraped knee and empty ice cream cone, he isn't so sure he can walk away, even if it is the best thing for her.

Harper might have vowed to cut all romance from her life, but Doc knows what she needs, and he's going to be the one to give it to her.

Shadowridge Guardians MC
Steele
Kade
Atlas
Doc
Gabriel
Talon
Bear
Faust
Storm

Combining the sizzling talents of bestselling authors Pepper North, Kate Oliver, and Becca Jameson, the Shadowridge Guardians are guaranteed to give you a thrill and leave you dreaming of your own throbbing motorcycle joyride.

Are you daring enough to ride with a club of rough, growly, commanding men? The protective Daddies of the Shadowridge Guardians Motorcycle Club will stop at nothing to ensure the safety and protection of everything that belongs to them: their Littles, their club, and their town. Throw in some sassy, naughty, mischievous women who won't hesitate to serve their fair share of attitude even in the face of looming danger, and this brand new MC Romance series is ready to ignite!

ALSO BY BECCA JAMESON

Roses and Thorns:

Marigold

Oleander

Jasmine

Tulip

Daffodil

Lily

Shadowridge Guardians:

Steele by Pepper North

Kade by Kate Oliver

Atlas by Becca Jameson

Doc by Kate Oliver

Gabriel by Becca Jameson

Talon by Pepper North

Blossom Ridge:

Starting Over

Finding Peace

Building Trust

Feeling Brave

Embracing Joy

Accepting Love

Blossom Ridge Box Set One

Blossom Ridge Box Set Two

The Wanderers:

Sanctuary

Refuge

Harbor

Shelter

Hideout

Haven

Surrender:

Raising Lucy

Teaching Abby

Leaving Roman

Choosing Kellen

Pleasing Josie

Honoring Hudson

Nurturing Britney

Charming Colton

Convincing Leah

Rewarding Avery

Surrender Box Set One

Surrender Box Set Two

Surrender Box Set Three

Open Skies:

Layover

Redeye

Nonstop

Standby

Takeoff

Jetway

Open Skies Box Set One

Open Skies Box Set Two

Shadow SEALs:

Shadow in the Desert

Shadow in the Darkness

Holt Agency:

Rescued by Becca Jameson

Unchained by KaLyn Cooper

Protected by Becca Jameson

Liberated by KaLyn Cooper

Defended by Becca Jameson

Unrestrained by KaLyn Cooper

Delta Team Three (Special Forces: Operation Alpha):

Destiny's Delta

Canyon Springs:

Caleb's Mate

Hunter's Mate

Corked and Tapped:

Volume One: Friday Night

Volume Two: Company Party

Volume Three: The Holidays

Project DEEP:

Reviving Emily

Reviving Trish

Reviving Dade

Reviving Zeke

Reviving Graham
Reviving Bianca
Reviving Olivia
Project DEEP Box Set One
Project DEEP Box Set Two

SEALs in Paradise:
Hot SEAL, Red Wine
Hot SEAL, Australian Nights
Hot SEAL, Cold Feet
Hot SEAL, April's Fool
Hot SEAL, Brown-Eyed Girl

Dark Falls:
Dark Nightmares

Club Zodiac:
Training Sasha
Obeying Rowen
Collaring Brooke
Mastering Rayne
Trusting Aaron
Claiming London
Sharing Charlotte
Taming Rex
Tempting Elizabeth
Club Zodiac Box Set One
Club Zodiac Box Set Two
Club Zodiac Box Set Three

The Art of Kink:

Pose

Paint

Sculpt

Arcadian Bears:

Grizzly Mountain

Grizzly Beginning

Grizzly Secret

Grizzly Promise

Grizzly Survival

Grizzly Perfection

Arcadian Bears Box Set One

Arcadian Bears Box Set Two

Sleeper SEALs:

Saving Zola

Spring Training:

Catching Zia

Catching Lily

Catching Ava

Spring Training Box Set

The Underground series:

Force

Clinch

Guard

Submit

Thrust

Torque

The Underground Box Set One

The Underground Box Set Two

Wolf Masters series:

Kara's Wolves

Lindsey's Wolves

Jessica's Wolves

Alyssa's Wolves

Tessa's Wolf

Rebecca's Wolves

Melinda's Wolves

Laurie's Wolves

Amanda's Wolves

Sharon's Wolves

Wolf Masters Box Set One

Wolf Masters Box Set Two

Claiming Her series:

The Rules

The Game

The Prize

Claiming Her Box Set

Emergence series:

Bound to be Taken

Bound to be Tamed

Bound to be Tested

Bound to be Tempted

Emergence Box Set

The Fight Club series:

Come

Perv

Need

Hers

Want

Lust

The Fight Club Box Set One

The Fight Club Box Set Two

Wolf Gatherings series:

Tarnished

Dominated

Completed

Redeemed

Abandoned

Betrayed

Wolf Gatherings Box Set One

Wolf Gathering Box Set Two

Durham Wolves series:

Rescue in the Smokies

Fire in the Smokies

Freedom in the Smokies

Durham Wolves Box Set

Stand Alone Books:

Blind with Love

Guarding the Truth

Out of the Smoke

Abducting His Mate

Wolf Trinity

Frostbitten

A Princess for Cale / A Princess for Cain

Severed Dreams

Where Alphas Dominate

ABOUT THE AUTHOR

Becca Jameson is a USA Today best-selling author of over 125 books. She is well-known for her Wolf Masters series, her Fight Club series, and her Surrender series. She currently lives in Houston, Texas, with her husband and her Goldendoodle. Two grown kids pop in every once in a while too! She is loving this journey and has dabbled in a variety of genres, including paranormal, sports romance, military, and BDSM.

A total night owl, Becca writes late at night, sequestering herself in her office with a glass of red wine and a bar of dark chocolate, her fingers flying across the keyboard as her characters weave their own stories.

During the day--which never starts before ten in the morning!--she can be found jogging, running errands, or reading in her favorite hammock chair!

…where Alphas dominate…

Becca's Newsletter Sign-up

Join my Facebook fan group, Becca's Bibliomaniacs, for the most up-to-date information, random excerpts while I work, giveaways, and fun release parties!

Facebook Fan Group:
Becca's Bibliomaniacs

Contact Becca:
www.beccajameson.com
beccajameson4@aol.com

facebook.com/becca.jameson.18
twitter.com/beccajameson
instagram.com/becca.jameson
bookbub.com/authors/becca-jameson
goodreads.com/beccajameson
amazon.com/author/beccajameson